More Critical Praise for Marlon James

for *John Crow's Devil*:

- Finalist for the *Los Angeles Times* Book Prize
- Finalist for the Commonwealth Writers' Prize

"A powerful first novel . . . Writing with assurance and control, James uses his small-town drama to suggest the larger anguish of a postcolonial society struggling for its own identity."
— *New York Times Book Review* (Editors' Choice)

"Elements coalesce in a Jamaican stew spicier than jerk chicken. First novelist James moves effortlessly between lyrical patois and trenchant observations . . . It's 150-proof literary rum guaranteed to intoxicate and enchant. Highly recommended."
— *Library Journal* (*starred* review)

"Set in James's native Jamaica, this dynamic, vernacular debut sings of the fierce battle between two flawed preachers . . . An exciting read."
— *Publishers Weekly*

"A mesmerizing treatise on the nature of good and evil, faith and madness, guilt and forgiveness, eloquently captured in a microcosm of society."
— *Booklist*

"*John Crow's Devil* is the finest and most important first novel I've read in years. His writing brings to mind early Toni Morrison, Jessica Hagedorn, and Gabriel García Márquez. While he writes about the travails of a small Jamaican town still struggling to unfasten the yoke of its colonial past, the issues and themes James raises are universal, and hugely relevant in the world today. Under the guise of self-righteous religiou~ f~   ~vil is done here; but as James so wisely poi~*~   ~e self-imprisonment of the mind—perpe~   ~r."
— Kaylie Jone~   ~*ever Cries*

"James's compelling story is told pa~   ~~an vernacular from the point of view of the townspeo~   ~ ~pproach that recalls Faulkner's 'A Rose for Emily.'"
— *Chicago Reader*

"Marlon James is the Sean Paul of the literary world, stirring up a firestorm in the international community."
— *Caribbean Beat*

"Marlon James masterfully challenges his audience's moral values and religious beliefs . . . This novel is necessary and provocative and his sophomore effort should be eagerly anticipated." —*Urbanology*

"A great first novel." —*Counterpoise*

"Literature needs more like him." —*Mosaic*

"Marlon is a brilliant writer who weaves a story that sends you on a rollercoaster of emotions—at times shocking, humorous, and leaving you with food for thought and discovery . . . If you only read one book for the rest of the year, this should be it." —*Sunday Herald* (Jamaica)

"*John Crow's Devil* is literally good to the last drop, when the suspense is unraveled in a plot that appears as winding as a country road in St. Andrew." —*Sunday Gleaner* (Jamaica)

"*John Crow's Devil* is a sober, and sobering, reflection on Christian values and human motives wrapped up in a classic good-vs.-evil story." —*Jamaica Observer*

"A very good novel by any standard, it combines sound, occasionally luminous prose, a compelling plot, and convincing characterization. One reluctantly has to concede that, for once, the blurbs in the author's publicity material don't sound faked." —*Caribbean Review of Books*

"*Pile them up*, a Marlon James character says repeatedly, and Marlon does just that. Pile them up: language, imagery, technique, imagination. All fresh, all exciting. This is a writer to watch out for." —Chris Abani, author of *GraceLand* and *Song for Night*

"*John Crow's Devil* is the kind of stylistically mature first novel that often comes at the beginning of an enduring career." —Colin Channer, best-selling author of *The Girl with the Golden Shoes*

"Marlon James spins his magical web in this novel and we willingly suspend disbelief, rewarded by the window he opens to Jamaica (and a world) rarely portrayed in fiction." —Elizabeth Nunez, author of *Anna In-Between*

for *The Book of Night Women*:

"Beautifully written and devastating . . . An undeniable success."
—*New York Times* (Editors' Choice)

"Not merely a historical novel, It's a canticle of love and hate."
—*Los Angeles Times*

"Hard to pick up, even harder to put down."
—*Chicago Tribune*

"An explosion of poetry, recalling the lyrical experiments of James Joyce, William Faulkner, Toni Morrison, and Irvine Welsh."
—*Washington Post*

"*The Book of Night Women* does what good fiction is uniquely situated to do—it revisits and reinvents the past in order to expose and indict inhumanity and hypocrisy. James also manages to be equally attentive in his nuanced renderings of compassion and hope."
—BookSlut

"It stands in the wake of Toni Morrison's transcendent slave literature, and it holds its own."
—*Cleveland Plain Dealer*

"The author has carved strong and compelling female figures out of the harsh landscape of nineteenth-century British-ruled Jamaica."
—*Miami Herald*

"An epic novel of late-eighteenth-century West Indian slavery, complete with all its carnage and brutishness, but one that, like a Toni Morrison novel, whispers rather than shouts its horrors."
—*Time Out New York*

"A stunning testament to the dynamics of ultimate power and powerlessness, *The Book of Night Women* will keep readers up at night."
—*Bookmarks*

"Marlon James's *The Book of Night Women* is a devastating epic of savage history, relentless oppression, and souls that refuse to be shackled."
—*Boston Globe*

john crow's devil

marlon james

This is a work of fiction. All names, characters, places, and incidents are the product of the author's imagination. Any resemblance to real events or persons, living or dead, is entirely coincidental.

Published by Akashic Books
©2005, 2010 Marlon James

ISBN-13: 978-1-936070-10-7
Library of Congress Control Number: 2009939040
Fourth paperback printing

Akashic Books
Brooklyn, New York, USA
Ballydehob, Co. Cork, Ireland
Twitter: @AkashicBooks
Facebook: AkashicBooks
E-mail: info@akashicbooks.com
Website: www.akashicbooks.com

To Ché, that other revolutionary,
and to my mother, who must not read this book.

Big Up

I wish to express my sincere thanks to all the following, who taught me that contrary to the name below the title, one person does not a book make:

Kaylie Jones, my editor, mentor, and friend, who saved this novel in a way that I will reveal one day; Colin Channer, Kwame Dawes, Justine Henzell, and Calabash; Elizabeth Nunez; Charlotte Wasserstein; victims who read the first draft of the manuscript: Danielle Goodman and Kwesi Dickson; Johnny Temple; everybody at Hallin Bank; the Cowans; James Hill Family; Clint and Elizabeth Hill; Ingrid Riley; Simon Levy; the Jameses, Dillons, and Messados; and any deserving person I completely forgot.

Three little children
With doves on their shoulders
They're countin out the Devil
With two fingers on their hands

—"Dachau Blues," Captain Beefheart

THE END

n o living thing flew over the village of Gibbeah, neither fowl, nor dove, nor crow. Yet few looked above, terrified should an omen come in a shriek or flutter. Nothing flew but dust. It slipped through window blades, door cracks, and the lifting clay of rooftops. Dust coated house and ground, shed and tree, machine and vehicle with a blanket of gray. Dust hid blood, but not remembrance.

Apostle York took three days to decide. He had locked himself in the office as his man waited by the door. Clarence touched his face often without thought, running his fingers over scratches hardened by clotted blood. The Apostle's man was still in church clothes: his one black suit and gray shirt with tan buttons that matched his skin, save for his lips, which would have been pink had they not been beaten purple three days ago. Clarence shifted from one leg to the other and squeezed his knuckles to prevent trembling, but it was no use.

"Clarence," the Apostle called from behind the door. "Pile them up. Pile them all up. Right where the roads meet. Pile them up and burn them."

Men, women, and children, all dead, were left in the road. Those who scurried home with their lives imprisoned themselves behind doors. There were five bodies on Brillo Road; the sixth lay with a broken neck in a ditch where the bridge used to be. Clarence limped, cursing the hop and drag of his feet. At the crossroads he stopped.

"All man who can hear me!" he shouted. "Time now to do the Lord's work. The Apostle callin you."

Faces gathered at windows but doors remained shut. Some would look at Clarence, but most studied the sky. Clarence looked above once and squeezed his knuckles again. A dove had flown straight into his face, splitting his bottom lip and almost scratching out his left eye. He felt as if more would come at that very moment, but the Apostle had given him strength.

"I talkin to every man who can stand. Heed the word or you goin get lick with friggery worse than any bird."

Birds. They came back in a rush; in screams and screeches and wounds cut fresh by claws.

"You know what my Apostle can do."

Clarence knew the houses where men hid. He hopped and dragged to each one and hammered into the door.

"Sunset," he said.

Three days before, when noon was most white, the village had killed Hector Bligh. Reckoning came swift, before they were even done. God's white fury swept down on them with beaks and claws and the beat of a thousand wings.

But there were things the villagers feared more than birds. One by one they came out and the men threw the bodies on the bonfire.

"This was judgment," said Apostle York. He had emerged from the office after the fire was lit. The Apostle's face had no scratch. "Judgment!" he shouted over the brilliance of the pyre and the crackle and pop of burning flesh. "Judgment," he said again in morning devotion, noon devotion, evening devotion, night mass, penitence prayer, children's prayer, women's prayer, blood atonement, prayer for the saints, and the School of Boy Prophets. From that day, the incident was never to be spoken of lest God again unleash his wrath on Gibbeah.

The building had begun a week before the killing. With chopped down trees the villagers made a fence all around Gibbeah's boundary. Then they surrounded it in barbed wire. Every city of righteousness had a wall, said the Apostle. This was God's way of keeping holiness in and iniquity out. Sooner than expected, the fence was finished. It wouldn't be long before nature hid wood and wire in the deceit of leaves, vines, and flowers. Soon Gibbeah would disappear from the map of men. Soon all would be spared from recollection but Lucinda.

She had also spent three days in a room, but her door was locked from the outside. Lucinda panicked whenever she trapped fingers in her gorgon hair.

Her eyes popped from jet skin. She had believed the Apostle, for love and God had punished her for sin. Before she went mad there were two faces in the mirror, neither of them hers. After Hector Bligh's death there were three. Bligh's eyes snaked her. They tormented her in dreams. She screamed at him in the tiny room below the church's steeple. The room stank of bird flesh. In a fit of rage brought on by the fever that madness carried, she struck the mirror and shattered it. But in each broken piece was another face. Three faces became ten, then a hundred and a thousand and still more. A million eyes that saw everything and judged like God. She could do nothing but scream. By day her room was dark, but at night she moved back and forth in the light, a gaunt silhouette one instant, a ragged chiaroscuro the next.

Human ash became dust. What dust would not cover, wind swept away. Gibbeah built a wall that sealed the village from memory. But within her walls Lucinda would not forget. His ghost lived with her now, his voice mimicked her cries, and his eyes saw her secret skin. The Apostle had called Hector Bligh a disgrace, abomination, and Antichrist.

She called him the Rum Preacher.

PART ONE

THE RUM PREACHER

make we tell you bout the Rum Preacher. Even if you never live anywhere near them parts, you must did hear bout the Rum Preacher. After six years, false story and true story rub together so much that both start shine. People think that everything shoot to Hell after the Devil take hold of Lillamae Perkins, but if you did know Pastor Hector Bligh of the Holy Sepulchral Full Gospel Church of St. Thomas Apostolic, you would know him was on the road to Hell long before that.

Before Pastor Bligh come to Gibbeah nobody ever see a man of God drink. Some people say Second Book of John, verse one to eleven, say that Jesus turn water into wine, so him must did drink wine too. Three man who sit down outside the bar all day say that him is man after all and man have right to get drunk just as him have right to scratch him balls when him want to scratch him balls or beat him woman when she don't act right.

Bligh drink like drinking goin out of style. All Saturday night when him should be readying himself for church, him down the bar drinking liquor and talking out people business. And when the time come to do the preaching, him don't know what to say. We never see preaching like this yet. When Bligh drunk all you hear is mumble. When Bligh dry him sound like that mad captain in that Moby Dick picture that show at the Majestic. The preacher before him did have fire. Hector Bligh have nothing but ice. Maybe is fi we fault cause country people take things as them be, as if white man goin beat we if we change them.

Lillamae.

Lillamae Perkins. Is was two years since the morning her father wake up but just for a minute to see him bed all red and blood gushing like spring from where him penis used to hang. Nobody never see what happen, but everybody see Lillamae, outside her gate looking like them obeah her, with one hand holding the knife and the other hand holding the bloody cocky. She eat green pawpaw to kill out the baby. Two years later, Sunday come and Pastor Bligh was him usual drunk self. Him fling himself into the Pastor seat by the pulpit like him would crash on the floor if him did miss. Lillamae goin up to the altar to have them drive out her sin and iniquity, even though Preacher never call nobody yet.

Everybody hear she.

"Lawd Jesus Christ! Lawd Jesus Christ! Consuming Fire! Consuming Fire! LAAAAAAAAAWD!!!"

Lillamae Perkins fling herself pon the ground. Her leg turn into scissors, she swing them open, then close, then open, and everybody could see her fishy which never cover up with no panty. Then she see Lucinda, who scream out to Holy Jesus Christ.

"Wha Jesus goin do fi you, river-whore? Satan watching you from you start mix tea," Lillamae say. People screaming and running, and tripping and crushing and more screaming, cause when she open her mouth is a man voice come out. Then she see the Pastor and all Hell break loose.

Five deacon rush the altar. Churchgoer and sinner both call them "The Five."

"One idiot, two drunkard, one sick-fowl, and one who beat woman. Now who is who? Who is who?" is what she say. The Five circle her, wrestle her, but nobody could pin down Lillamae. She slip from one like grease and claw through another one face. She kick a deacon in him seed bag and five man become four. Lillamae beat up all of them. She crick the second man neck, break all of the third man finger, punch asthma back into the fourth man chest, and blind the last deacon in him left eye.

Nobody know where the knife come from. Some people say she jump, some people say she fly. When demon take you, you can do anything. All people see is when she leap after the Pastor with the knife and him hold out him hand like him was goin catch her and she stab right through him left hand middle and him stuck on the wall like Holy Jesus crucified.

"Fool. You should a do this two years ago when we was one. Now we is one and seven," was all she say. Pastor Bligh bawling and screaming, but nobody goin cross a girl with eight demon in her. Then she scream and run out of the church.

Two day pass and nobody can find Lillamae. Then Wednesday, a little boy find her body sailing down Two Virgins River. Pastor Bligh did drunk when him bury her. After that plenty people stop come to church.

Coming home from the bar, Pastor Bligh made his way up the road, teetering like a drunken colossus. But the fire dug holes in his gut and sent flame down his thighs screaming, *Let me out!* He moved over to the side of the road and released himself, bursting a black circle on the pavement with a torrent of yellow piss. The sun teased him from behind and suddenly there was lightness to the morning. He had learned long ago never to trust happiness. But something came over him, bringing both pleasure and a slight fear. A silliness that made him fall in love with pink-striped skies and opalescent dew bubbles and chickens crowing themselves awake. Bligh was still very much drunk. His pants were around his ankles and when he moved he tripped, fell backwards on the base of his skull, and knocked himself out.

A church sister saw him first. She had come out to water her hibiscus and thought a mad man or a drunkard had fallen dead in the road. She inched toward him, afraid that he was merely asleep and would awake at that very second to rape her with calloused hands and dirty fingernails. But when she saw Pastor Bligh's face, the woman frowned, disgusted and unsurprised. "Disgrace" she said. And yet she was relieved by Pastor Bligh's behavior, as were many in the village. So tormented was he by his own sin that he could never convict them of theirs. But as she summed him up from head to foot, her view came to a halt midway. There looking at her was his dark penis and balls, sprawled as carelessly as he was, bracketed by his thighs and the open ends of his shirt. She forgot his arms; the right spread open and the left under his back. She forgot his face, gaunt and gray, his mouth open and pooling with drool. She forgot his shoes, dirty, brown, and mostly covered by pants that strangled his ankles. There was only the thing, lifeless between two legs yet as monstrous as a serpent in Genesis. Her dark face went white, even pink, as she rushed back to her house. For several minutes he was unconscious.

Minutes that horrified old women and scandalized children who passed by on the way to school. Lucinda, who never witnessed the incident, would nonetheless report of it in the first person in that tone she reserved for special heresies.

After the pee-pee incident, the concerned citizens of the village, namely Lucinda, had had enough.

"Him goin mistake him chair for a toilet next Sunday, just watch," said one observer, but as he was not a member of the church no one heard, anticipated, or dreaded it. In short, that person was not Lucinda, who had begun a letter-writing campaign to have Pastor Bligh removed. Lucinda remembered very little schooling other than the Bible, so her words often packed more Hellfire and damnation than she intended. She wrote to every church she knew, even the archdiocese, despite Pastor Bligh being no Catholic. Bligh answered to nobody but God, and Jesus wasn't saying anything that Lucinda wanted to hear.

Nobody answered Lucinda's letters. She would never curse God, but reminded Him that this was why she also prayed to someone else. Then the Majestic Cinema started showing Sunday matinees at 10:00 and chopped the halved congregation to a quarter. The Pastor now drank day and night. He was spiraling downward and would have taken the village with him were it not for the other, who lead them instead to a light blacker than the thickest darkness.

He came like a thief on a night colored silver. He came on two wheels, the muffler puffing a mist that made children cough in their sleep. As his motorcycle coursed up Brillo Road it left a serpentine trail of dust. There were no witnesses to his coming, save for an owl, the moon, and the Devil.

You say you saw it coming, Yea
But still you did not flee

—"Splints," Sixteen Horsepower

THE PREACHER AND THE APOSTLE

A murder of crows came first. Hundreds. From no point of origin they blackened the sun, forming a shifty eclipse that descended on Gibbeah. The birds flew up the road in a parade of darkness, their wings cutting through the wind and scaring even the smallest children. As a few landed in the road their red necks exposed them. Not ravens, but vultures. Country people called them John Crows. Several more landed and hopped and hobbled, picking through garbage as they overthrew the village. As soon as they saw people the birds would tilt their heads and frown, looking curious and angry. Between the John Crows and the village began a horrific game of wait.

Then they took off. A chorus of flutters, louder than before, flew from roof to roof as if shaking loose evil spirits. Then nothing. The morning began to assert herself. Routine returned.

Brillo Road cut through the village like the trunk of a crucifix. Hanover Road sat near the top, completing the cross. From above the village looked like a squashed hot cross bun. This was Gibbeah.

The Astor Sugar Plantation was nearly thirty miles away. When slaves were finally set free in 1838, they were evicted as well. The white missionaries who pursued emancipation for the negro nonetheless recoiled at the thought of one in the dining room, boardroom, or bedroom of anyone white. They established free villages all over the island, Gibbeah being one. The freed slaves had their own land but no money or food. One year after the death of slavery, the ex-slaves were back on the plantation willingly contributing to its rebirth.

And yet the plantation died, wounded by a dastard class of white men who fled back to the mother country. The ones who stayed either denied or reveled in their decline as fields dried up or were taken over by land reform. Neighbors disappeared; the mother country enforced Crown Colony government, and lesser suitors like beet dethroned King Sugar. In their place rose a new breed of white man who was sometimes black. They were merchants, machine men, and dealers, men who brought the Americans. Men who turned plantations into guesthouses or hotels if they were near the sea. Moneymaking shifted to a new kind of Massa. Men like Aloysius Garvey.

By 1928, Mr. Aloysius Garvey had bought, built, and owned most of the land. He renamed the village Garveyville, but everybody kept on calling it Gibbeah. He was a thin man, almost skeletal, even when he was young, with negro lips and dark skin at war with his hooked nose and straight hair. Though a black bastard unacknowledged by his white father, he still had a birthright to money. But he was a man out of time with neither wife nor peer. His large red house, built like a plantation's Great House, stood at the top of Brillo Road and stank of death. With a cut-stone ground floor and a wooden floor on top, the house was crowned with an arch roof and garnished with astrological fretwork. French windows held dark curtains that revealed no secrets. In time and with grime, people forgot that the house was red and called it black. There was a rumor that he was a sodomite and there was the matter of his several light-skinned nephews, but word was wind in Gibbeah.

Mr. Aloysius Garvey, being the owner of the village, declared how he wanted Gibbeah to look. In 1928, he made all houses face the street and painted them rusty red. During Lent when there was drought, dirt would stick to the walls and the village would seem as if trapped in the eye of a dust storm. The houses were all alike, with creaky verandahs and double doors that opened into a small living room with bedrooms flanking both sides. The living room, which was really a hallway, led into the dining room, which some used as the living room. To the left of the dining room was the kitchen. Piped water came twenty-three years later when Bligh did in 1951. There were only two roads in Gibbeah. Mr. Garvey had the idea to build the houses along the pattern of the crossroads, but he could not stop the others, the squatters, from building rickety shacks as they saw fit. Still, when the new houses popped up, they took on the colors of the old ones. Gibbeah was bordered by a river, which swung around the village in a circle like a moat. The bridge was the only way in or out.

~~§~~

Ash Wednesday morning had come and the crows were gone. This was one of five mornings when Mr. Garvey went out in public, except for the funerals of those of stature or those who died under tragic circumstances. Funeral was spectacle in Gibbeah. Black clothing was foreign and expensive, sent over to the village in barrels from relatives living in America, England, or Panama. They were winter clothes, velvets, corduroys, denims, and wools that would conspire with the sun to bake the wearer while sucking his sweat. But there was no spectacle like the Garvey procession. Marching in slow step like pall-bearers without a coffin, Mr. Garvey with his nephews in one line behind him would take the left row at the front of the church. He would sit near the window, not bothering to take off his maroon hat with pink trim even in church, and his nephews would fill out the row in descending order of height. Some would gossip that they sat in descending order of color, with the lightest child beside Mr. Garvey and the darkest by the aisle, so that he could be the closest to black people. Before the service was over, he would rise, run his thin fingers over his black pin-striped suit, and his nephews would rise as well. In a line they would leave, the youngest nephew in front and Mr. Garvey in the back, who would toss some money at the altar and march through the door, his coattails flapping in the breeze. But this Ash Wednesday, as church was about to start, there was no sign of Mr. Garvey. Many were curious, but most were like Lucinda, who dismissed such things. Naturally, a man who was so rich that he made black white, would sooner or later stop coming to black people church. Especially a sodomite who was on his way to Hell. Country people took his absence as they took everything else.

But this morning the Rum Preacher was sober. Many forgot how tall he actually was, so like Gregory Peck midway between *Roman Holiday* and *Moby Dick*, which were still shown as a double feature at the Majestic. Pastor Bligh was wiry, a giant in the village. But disgrace diminished him. Guilt threw a curve in his back and a hunch in his stance. He had a square jaw with thick eyebrows over thin eyes and short, graying hair that was white at the temples. He was not a dark man, but not light either. His color was a nebulous thing, so like his voice, which was too low to be weak but too reedy to be commanding. In a town that preferred things black or white, grayness such as his was not welcome.

Bligh refused friendship. His sermons even when he was sober rocked with the terror and uncertainty of a man not in control. When the spirit came over him, he was racked without mercy, and left with sweat and tremors. Outside church they avoided him, lest the spirit assail him at that very moment and God punish them too. Sin, guilt, conviction, and redemption: things he may have spoke of, but always carried in the shakiness of his voice.

The church service began at 8:15. The sun was subdued by a mob of reddish gray clouds. Wind slammed the church doors shut. She whispered and taunted through door spaces and half closed windows. Then the doors swung open and wind rushed in, knocking off hats and veils and sweeping up skirts and dresses. For a few seconds the church went to pieces. The wind forced herself all the way up to the altar and knocked over the Pastor's water glass, which fell on the purple carpet but did not break. Then she vanished.

The organist raised a hymn and within seconds the usual people were at the altar praying, praising, and yelling. Pastor Bligh had a word today. The word was flesh before he was flesh. Not his to claim, just to say. This was a burden he felt unfit for, but what right had he to the anguish of the major prophets? He was humbled that God had tolerated him for so long. But God was leading and he had to follow. Duty, then, not pleasure or purpose. He stood up, without having to correct his balance, and sung with the church.

It soon be done
All my trouble and trial
When I get home
On the other side
I'm gonna shake my hands with the elders
I'm gonna tell all the people good morning
I'm gonna sit down beside my Jesus
I'm gonna sit down and rest a little while!

The church was caught up in chorus singing and Hallelujah shouting. Women and men were dancing before the Lord and confessing his greatness. From the back of the half filled church came a sound like the crash of a tambourine. But from the front, the shattered stained glass window fell like rain. One of the John Crows from before had flown into the window, bursting through like a bullet, exploding in multicolored glass and blood. The organist saw nothing but the choir panicked. Lucinda screamed as the John Crow landed dead on the pulpit. Disgusted, those at the altar went back to their seats. Pastor Bligh instructed The Five to remove the vulture. They hesitated. John Crows were messengers of the Devil—everybody knew it. The Pastor kicked the vulture from the pulpit to the floor. One of The Five took the bird through the door, leaving a trail of blood spatter.

"Wickedness. God sent Jonah to warn Nineveh about wickedness," Hector Bligh said. "Elijah warned Ahab. John warned Herod. But nobody listens to the man of God. They burn him. They stab him, they whip him, and they chop off his head. They crucify him. They kill the messenger and spit out the message like a bitter orange seed. Everybody kills the messenger, nobody hears the message."

The congregation had been here before. When he was drunk, Bligh's sermon jumped from several points in the Bible at once and collapsed under convoluted scripture. When he was sober, he began in a sonorous mumble that grew to a sharp, bitter echo by the end. They had stopped listening to him, but he had stopped preaching to them. He spoke without pause for thought, preaching not to man or God or even himself. He accepted this as easily as he did all defeat. Bligh's eyes swept the room to see a congregation looking but not seeing, all but one.

"Something's coming. Something's coming. Coming on mighty wings. I'm sorry for who not ready. This is not what I came to preach. I came to preach about forgiveness. The Lord had other . . . This is what Jesus told me to tell you.

"There are those among you not ready. There are those among you, if you died right now, will roast in the lake of fire. If the rapture comes tonight you'll be swinging from a tree like Judas Iscariot. Satan coming like a roaring lion and he's going to devour you unless you let the Lord come dwell in you. Unless you come back the Lord. There are those among you grieving the Holy Spirit. You need to purify your heart before it's too late. Satan coming like a roaring lion.

"Whosoever want God healing stream, come to the altar. Tomorrow might be too late. God's vengeance is swift and brutal. Nobody will escape the white throne of Judgment."

Seven minutes later a man rose from his seat and went to the altar. His huge frame and squeaky army boots cut through the stillness of the church. The organist played "Closer Than a Brother My Jesus Is to Me." The choir hummed. Soon a girl rose, and another, a woman. The altar, easy to approach for praise, was difficult to approach for forgiveness. Church people, through their stares, created a boundary of shame that few climbed over. But then another man stood up, and three more women. Then a child. Lucinda had no choice. She missed her favorite spot, to the right of the podium, that bore the permanent dent of her knees. She scowled. Pastor Bligh prayed.

"Father, forgive our trespasses as we forgive those who trespass against us!"

He watched from the back of the church. The man had come with the night but darkness stayed with him in day. He was unnerved by all the excitement. The feeling was as strange as ecstasy or remorse. A fat day or a thin year carried the same weight if one had the same hate. He was taller than the Pastor, with black shoes, black suit, black shirt, black hair, and light skin that the sun had roasted. The altar called him and he made his way. Behind bent knees and prostrate bodies, he stood. The Pastor did not see him at first, but then gaze met gaze and Hector Bligh blinked. Bligh looked away and continued to declare his flock free. But the man's eyes followed him. He stretched his arms wide and stepped toward the Pastor's podium. A space cleared as if the church had been waiting for him. The Pastor noticed. The man shut his eyes, but looked upward, as if to a Heaven higher than the Pastor's. Hector Bligh hesitated before approaching him; admonishing himself that fear was not of God. But surprise was to play no role in this incident. So when the Pastor laid hands on the man in black and he pushed them away, there was no aback to be taken. This was no conflicted soul whose path he would make straight. He knew this but felt compelled to be pastorly. Hector Bligh placed his hands on the man's head but the man grabbed both, squeezing them to the bone. He made little effort. Hector Bligh knew he was weak, but never before had his weakness been made so manifest.

"So who's going to forgive you? Who's going to forgive all of you?"

Bligh did not understand the intimacy. This demon had the wrong man. The man tightened the grip on his arms and agony shot through his shoulders.

"Who's going to forgive you, you ignorant son of a bitch?"

The man grabbed Pastor Bligh at the sides.

"Who's going to wash away *your* sin? Who's going to purify you of *your* unrighteousness? Who's going to make *you* as white as snow?"

He flung the Pastor into the wall behind him. As he slammed into the bricks, Bligh felt the wind forced out of his lungs. But the man in black was not done. The organist stopped and the congregation was still.

The Five stormed the pulpit, eager to unleash the violence that brimmed in church muscle. The man had gone over to the Pastor and grabbed him by his robes. The Five circled him, about to pounce, but then he raised his hand and pointed two fingers. The men stopped, lunging forward in momentum, but with their feet firm on the floor. They knew they were not frozen. They knew they could walk if they chose to. The Five thought it ridiculous, crazy that this strange man had commanded them without words like they were cows, but none dared move. Someone in the congregation screamed. Another shouted. From the sea of grumbling rose curses and bellows, but then the man raised his hand again, pointed two fingers, and the congregation fell quiet.

Lawd a massy, you should a see it when all Hell break loose in the church!

Then pop story give we.

All we see is this man. First we think say is Devil. Then we think is Gabriel or Michael or one of them strong angel.

Tell we bout the Hell that break loose.

Yes me dear, the man set pon Pastor Bligh like when you a beat mangy dog. Caca-fart!

You understand? This yah man just grab Pastor like him make out o paper and fling him clear cross the pulpit. Any higher and him would a crash in the stain glass.

Christmas!

If ever. Then next thing you know the man set pon Pastor like demon. Him slap him so, then so, then so, then so again. Before you know it, Pastor a spit blood.

Rahtid!

But him never done. Him thump Pastor in him head, him slap Pastor cross him back, then him kick Pastor in him seed bag. Pastor face mash up. To think just before that the Pastor warning we bout Satan the roaring lion.

Shithouse!

Then him call Pastor three thing.

Three thing? What three thing?

First him call him Disgrace.

Which him is, thank you Jesus.

Then him call him Abominational.

Oh babababa—lekim—shakam!

Then him call him Antichrist. And him say it like this: ANTICHRIST.

Lawd Puppa Jesus!

Eehi. Then the man start speak in tongue, but is no Abba babba tongue, and him still a drop lick pon the Pastor.

What is this pon we Puppa Jesus!

The man grab Pastor Bligh like him is garbage and drag him out of the church himself. We see it with we own eye.

Hataclaps! But hi, a who this man be?

A week later, Lucinda would say that the Holy Spirit was moving in a powerful way. But in that moment, another spirit seemed to be moving through the pews. The man grew taller in those few minutes, and his voice bounced from roof to floor with authority. He could have been Gabriel or Michael or the Avenging Angel sent by God to tell them that He was not pleased. This was judgment on their lying, thieving, and whoring generation. A good thing, then, that Lucinda's body was blameless. But the man moved with so much darkness that she wondered if his soul was just as black. She cringed as the near-unconscious body of the Pastor was dragged past her. Bligh was muttering to himself, his left hand trailing on the floor and his right in the mighty grip of the man in black. He took Bligh down the aisle and through the church door that nobody remembered opening.

A week later, Lucinda proclaimed his appearance the work of Jesus, but back then she feared the working of another spirit, the one whom preachers called in a hushed voice *The Enemy*. Back in the church, she clutched herself and whispered an intercessory prayer, dreading yet yearning for the man's return. Yearning? A long-dead emotion stirred itself, which she rebuked in a flurry of Yes Lords. The church waited. Then he returned, emerging from outside as if the sun had birthed him. He was ruddy and handsome, mixed of black and white, or maybe light Indian or Creole Chinaman. His long, curly hair was unruly from beating Bligh, but Lucinda imagined that it was always that way. She smelt his fire and quickly made for her seat. He saw her as she fled.

"But Lucinda. My sister. Isn't this what you've been praying for? Aren't your fingers tired from writing? Don't those knees ache from kneeling, waiting on God?"

He touched her face and whispered, "Didn't He see you mixing tea til He came?"

Convicted and blessed in one fell swoop, she fell to the ground praying and weeping. The man stepped up to the pulpit and waved away The Five, who had been still up to that point. The congregation felt free as well and raised a rumble of whispers and half-said words. He raised his hand again and the church fell silent, save for Lucinda who praised the Lord for His consuming fire yet wondered how much the man in black knew. She shivered. How could he have heard about the tea? Lucinda brewed hidden weeds whenever she wore her secret skin at night.

"Who knows what just happened here?"

Silence.

"Anybody wants try a guess. No? Speak up, you were all yapping just a minute ago."

"Consuming fiiiiire."

"Victory. My Lord has blessed you with victory! Scream it from the highest highs, shout it from the lowest lows, Gibbeah, the Lord has heard your cry. The Lord has seen your suffering. That the body could survive for so long with that abomination as a head is only because of the grace of the One who made you.

"This church is a disgrace, I tell you. Disgrace, and you're all accountable for it. Did I say all? I stand corrected. The church is half empty. Obviously, the ones with sense are finding God somewhere else. Where did they go? Are they at home? In bed? In somebody else's bed? Stealing? Sinning? Well speak up, you all had mouth before.

"This is what the body of Christ has come to? Maybe it's not your fault. Maybe congregations do get the Pastors they deserve. Maybe you and him have a good thing going, eh? He doesn't try to save you, you don't try to damn him—oh yes! I know what has been going on here. Things that would make a sodomite blush.

"But God sent me. And the first thing we're going to do? Clean out this temple.

"Listen to me, Gibbeah. I've come to bring back integrity and smash out iniquity, Hallelujah. I've come to comfort the afflicted and afflict the comfortable. Gibbeah! I've come with a sword!"

He grabbed the podium and the congregation watched his face as the same lines that knotted in fury relaxed to warmth.

"When was the last time you saw God? Felt His presence? Heard His voice? When was the last time you entered His gates with thanksgiving and His courts with praise? You didn't see it, but I see it plainly. The Lord nearly packed his bags to quit this place.

"But God.

"Do you feel the spirit? Can you hear it? It's here. Revival. New vision. New revelation. I prophesy in His name. Can you feel it, my sister? Is it washing over you, my brother? I feel it. Everybody who is a child of the Lord should be feeling it right now. Right now!

"Yes church, this is a new day. A new era. You know what era means? It means something old gone and something new come. Oh yes.

"My name is York. Anybody knows the hymn, 'I'm So Glad?'"

DEAD NEPHEWS

He called himself Apostle York. And nothing that had yet invaded Gibbeah—not redifusion radio, Bazooka Joe chewing gum, or condoms—moved with his seismic force. He was a whirlwind. He was a center. Fluttery voices made mention of the Apostle's looks, so like Tyrone Power in *The Mask of Zorro* that was still shown at the Majestic, but with a trimmed beard, wet eyes, and unruly black hair, like a coolie. God had sent him to Gibbeah. Jesus looked just like him. This meant he had power to deal with Pastor Bligh as brashly as the Lord dealt with money changers in the Temple. Pastor Bligh, disrobed and disgraced, simply disappeared.

As a Pastor, nobody was sure of Hector Bligh's authority, but York was an Apostle. Like Peter and Paul, like somebody who knew Jesus. His certificate said so. Lucinda hung the framed paper in the office that she spent two days purging of Hector Bligh. She had helped the Apostle move; her steely resolve withered down to a meek, servile heart. Yet there was not much to move as the Apostle had taken next to nothing for his journey.

In five days, he had already brought a change in Lucinda. She relaxed the shoulders that were always tense, smoothed away the twist in her nose from her permanent frown. But Lucinda was uneasy. He mentioned tea only once but the moment nagged her still. She wondered how much he guessed and how much he knew. God never shared her secrets before.

Change was refiguring Gibbeah. Every village had a rhythm that revealed itself in the pace men walked and women talked. The change alarmed the old folk whose lives had been reduced to watching such things. The village hummed and whistled and whispered and shouted and laughed. Even the unsaved were caught up with meeting him. Even the drunkard men and loose women were curious about this Apostle York, the savior-killer of Holy Sepulchral Full Gospel Church of St. Thomas Apostolic. The man who had beaten and maybe even killed Pastor Bligh, then sent him to Hell. The man who made the Holy Ghost thunder.

Lucinda wiped the church clean of Hector Bligh. Hector *Blight*, she called him, and spat on the floor. She came with mop, bucket, detergent, and water. She came with a mind bent on riddance and a heart on restoration. Lucinda scrubbed the church clean herself, wiping to the melody of "Closer Than a Brother" riding side-saddle on "Swing Low Sweet Chariot." This was her work. This was her purpose. God told her to make paths straight and to make the church ready. She wiped the podium, mopped the altar floor, and rubbed the windows to such a sparkly sheen that sunlight slipped through and bounced off wooden benches. The office was next.

Clutter blackened the room. Light blue walls surrendered to the shadows of books, pictures, and maps. She opened the glass window and the dust woke up, swirling around her like demons. She cursed the Rum Preacher, whose smell the room carried, along with liquor and failure. Lucinda threw out every book not marked Bible. Two hours later the clean and spacey room gave her pause. The large mahogany desk reclaimed its splendor, commanding the center of the room. The chair stood waiting behind it. Bibles were returned to clean bookshelves that bracketed the desk on the right and left walls. Lucinda had washed and polished the floor until she could see her raw knuckles in the reflection. *Closer than a brother to swing low sweet chariot.* She brought in the Apostle's books, even though not told to do so, and caressed the ones she recognized: an American Bible and a Bible concordance. The rest, books of Maccabees and Wisdom, Notorious Arts and Hermetics, and some with no name, she puzzled over briefly, but stacked them confidently when she came across the name Solomon. "Wisdom is as wisdom does," she said. The office was ready.

"My word . . . Look at this! I tell you, Lucinda, you have a gift! A true gift! Lord bless you! I tell you, this place was going to Hell in a hand basket, but God just used His daughter. Yes He did, yes He did." He touched her forehead and pools of red welled up in her ebony brown cheeks.

"Tha . . . Pastor . . . I mean, Apostle. Pardon, sir." She left quickly, uncomfortable with a man she had already declared a spiritual force. An Apostle was so much more than a Pastor or a sinner.

"As you wish. Sunday, then." He grinned. Laugh lines interlocked with each other and weakened her knees.

"S—Sunday."

Behind the village and across the river Pastor Bligh was asleep. He fell behind dead coconut and banana trees, resting beneath a roof that had formed itself out of fallen branches. Ramshackle and weak, it threatened to fall at any moment. The Pastor felt the same way. Yet he tried not to feel. He was stubborn in believing that things were as God willed and only by accepting them would he find peace. Bligh had known this day would come, he saw it coming up from the bottom of a rum bottle. Vengeance was the Lord's, and God was exacting His. Hector Bligh's bruised face ached. His mind was restless, taking turns between guilt, confusion, and the shame at being found out. One could play at being a preacher for only so long before God stomped out such mockery with his feet. The river's tumult brought him to calm and he fell asleep.

Hector Bligh came to Gibbeah in 1951 and had been there six years. Many had heard of him, but nobody from Gibbeah. His father and brother both died in 1927, the father of a broken heart, the brother of a broken neck. Hector remembered the wide sweep of the marble floor and the ordered lines of tiles shattered by his brother's twisted body. He had fallen over the balcony. The housekeeper screamed at the sight. Looking up to the floor above, she saw Hector—naked, sweaty, with his penis still erect—and screamed again. In Hector's bedroom, crouched naked in a dark corner and sobbing, was his brother's wife. The ruffled bed was witness to their sin. He joined the seminary soon after.

Guilt drove Pastor Bligh's life. Failure that seemed constant and deliberate. Gibbeah was his eleventh parish in twenty years. Ten of those he'd spent in study, a relief to him given his failure as a preacher. Bligh's salvation record was the worst in the county. People would say that if the Rum Preacher was all that stood between Heaven and Hell, then everybody had better stock up on asbestos. There were some who wondered why a man as rich as Aloysius Garvey would hire someone as worthless as Pastor Bligh, but there were others who felt they already knew. Aloysius Garvey did not meddle in poor people's business, and poor people were not expected to meddle in his. The villagers paid rent by slipping the money in his letterbox, not by dealing with him personally. This was how things were done, and father and mother taught son and daughter the same way. Neither Mr. Garvey nor his nephews had been seen in weeks, so nobody expected to see him now, welcoming the Apostle. That was poor people business.

Something prodded Bligh's face searching for a way inside. He thought he was dreaming until the stick pushed itself between his lazy lips, hitting his teeth with blunt force. He woke up stunned, and the girl, the youngest of the three, screamed, terrified and thrilled that she had woken up the giant of the bush. *Him was sleeping but now him wake and him goin eat her and is her brother fault cause him dare her to do it.* The stick fell from his mouth as he rubbed his eyes. He heard them giggling. The Pastor was found.

Bligh brushed the crusty mud off his jacket and stood up. The rest of his body was still asleep. He hid behind the shadows of trees as the children ran away. By now, most of the houses, the ones on Brillo Road certainly, had running water so nobody had reason to come to the river anymore. She flowed slowly, a movement colored with dejection that matched his own. Bligh was forgotten. This was where demon girl Lillamae was found floating, and since then the river had a thing of death. What that thing was, nobody was really sure. Something that lived and did not in a state like a vapor, or a spirit, or a memory, or nothing at all. It was inevitable that this would be the place to find a dead girl, inevitable as Ophelia. Now the river was merely a boundary to keep good in and evil out.

His mind fought against him, trying to make sense of Sunday. But Bligh would not think of that day. This was why he drank, so that his mind could never rebel against itself. There were some in Gibbeah who wondered if he would ever grow tired of mockery and scorn, but Bligh never refused it. He accepted being thought of as simple, hopeless, even stupid. He accepted the whispers that went before him and the laughter that crept after. Bligh accepted these things because he knew that if they stopped whispering or laughing then they would start thinking. And if the villagers started to think they would realize that he had no business being a preacher. *A sinner playing a saint's game*, his brother's ghost would whisper every time he pulled the white and purple robes over his head.

Enough with thinking! Better to live by a tree and shit by the river. The Lord giveth and the Lord taketh away.

Before the week was out the village knew where to find Pastor Bligh.

Lawd a massy, Puttus, you no hear the latest bout the Pastor?

No! Is weh you a hide the secret for, pop the story give we!

Well, people say the Pastor deh down a river a live like mad man.

Holy Jesus our Heavenly Father.

True-true. Him deh down deh a live like dog. People say him all a shit down deh.

Then where people expect him fi shit?

We did think say the Apostle kill him.

Who say him no dead?

True-true, the Rum Preacher is nothing but duppy now, heh-hay!

Then you a go look?

No baba, who want to see that deh?

People who see him say when him head take him, him play wid him teeli.

Lawks, how people mouth so dutty! Plus, everybody in Gibbeah know that deh cocky already.

Then hi, Pastor Bligh a go stay down the river for the rest of him life?

We no know, why you no go ask him? Why him no go back where him come from, is what Christian people want to know.

Eehi. Way it seem, it shouldn't hard fi get back to where him come from.

How you figure so, since him no figure that out yet?

Easy! All him have to do is dig a hole deep enough and him is there, me chile. Home sweet home.

True-true. Be it ever so humble.

Be it what?

Lawks, you people no watch picture show? You ignorant, baba.

Ignorant like you, baba!

～√€○

The Pastor knew that everybody knew and everybody knew that the Pastor knew that everybody knew. Yet everybody acted as if they knew nothing; as if the secret was too terrible to share with the Apostle. The village bounced to a new rhythm as if Hector Bligh had never existed.

Sunday. Church was so full that Lucinda had The Five set up stackable chairs at the front and side doors. Some came to praise and worship, but most came to see. They sat and spoke and gossiped and laughed like penny stinkers. The choir raised praise songs and those who didn't know the words either hummed or stared at the ceiling, trapped in a moment that they had never been a part of. They clapped to songs that needed no clapping or stood quiet, hoping that silence would be read as reverence. Lucinda was already in front. Her arms were spread wide as she spun and spun and spun. But nobody had come to see her. They waited and he appeared. The Apostle's robes billowed even though there was no wind. Pastor Bligh's robes were white and purple. Lavender and bleach. Detergent and antiseptic. The Apostle's black and red robes blew with flesh and blood, terror and magnificence. The choir simmered down to "Amazing Grace" and he gripped the podium, overcome by the spirit.

"Oh Lord! Oh Heavenly Father! King of Kings and Lord of Lords! Save us for we are wretches, dear Lord! Of which I am the worst! Redeem us, mighty one! We were blind but now we see! Oh precious Lord!"

"Consuming fiiiiiiiiiiire! Consuming fiiiiiiiiiiire!"

"Hallelujah!"

"Praise the Lord! Praise the Lord!"

"Jesus!" came from a woman at the back. Before she sat down, a cough arose that would not go away. She patted her chest, but the cough harassed her throat. She doubled over.

"Lift up this congregation Lord, as we give you the highest praise! And the church shall say . . ."

"Amen."

"Come church, what kind of fenke-fenke Amen that? The Lord wants to smell the sweet fragrance of your praise. AND THE CHURCH SHALL SAY?"

"AMEN!"

The woman was still coughing. One of The Five took her outside, where she vomited. When there was nothing left to vomit she heaved and hacked and stumbled to the ground. The usher helped her up and she vomited again.

The congregation then sat down and the Apostle stared at them for several minutes, casting a curious eye at some, an indignant eye at others.

"Seems that so many of us are so—what's the word I'm looking for?—consumed, yes, *consumed* by holy fire that we just had to come to His house today, Amen? After all, it must be God that we've all come to see, eh, Clarence? So many of you looking, nobody really seeing, blind by what binds. I know why some of you are here. I know why most of you are here. You didn't come for the message, you came for the mess. But you know, praise God, He doesn't give a damn how you get into His presence, just as long as you get into Him."

"Hallelujah! Hallelujah!"

"But really now, I want to do something preposterous. Can I do it, church? Can I do it? Is that alright? Yes? Okay, everybody who wasn't in church last week, please stand up."

One by one they stood up at the back. The drunkards cursed themselves for being opened up to such shame. Even Christians were afraid of being made an example of. Some smiled smiles already weakened by embarrassment, some stared at the ground. Only a few looked at the Apostle, who held the moment for a few seconds. "Praise God. Church, today we're going to talk about lost sheep."

The Rum Preacher knew he would not be seen. That took no faith; he knew Gibbeah's love for spectacle. They were drawn to the Apostle, but he was drawn as well. He went all the way to the old cobblestone track that led up to the church steps, but grew heartsick as soon as he saw the steeple. He could go no farther.

"I tell you, church, it's up to you to bring every one of these lost sheep back. I can't do much. I can only minister against the sinister. It's up to you. Now understand me. I know it's not your fault why we losing sheep. It's his fault. You know of who I speak."

"Preach it, Preacher!"

"A preacher starts a church with ten members and dies with the same damn ten. But I'm not a preacher. I came with a sword. If you're not serving the Lord, you're serving the Devil. One or the other, until you die. So when you crawl out of a bed that is not yours, it can only be the Devil's work that you're doing. Can I get a witness, Clarence?"

Clarence felt his balls quiver.

"Lost sheep. Some of us don't want to be found. You ready for this secret, Gibbeah? This will make you tremble. Some of you are in the middle of the flock and still lost."

The snoring woman was shaken awake. She opened her eyes suddenly, aware of her awkwardness before she saw the pool of her own drool on the floor. A stream of it hung suspended from her bottom lip unawares to her. She collected herself, sat up straight, and opened her Bible like an eager student. When the tail of spit finally fell onto the page, she shut the Bible loudly and wiped her lip, darting glances left and right.

Pastor Bligh retreated to the river. Only she would welcome him now. Only a few days ago he had staggered under guilt and shame, but now he could not escape a feeling of lightness. What was this then, honesty rising up from the torpid waters of truth? Relief? The Lord giveth and the Lord taketh away. He was set to become Pastor from before his brother's death, so why should his life be bowed down by it still? Bligh accepted guilt as he did all things; condemned to live his brother's death over and over. His time and memory was as God's, without boundary. But why feel torment at being rejected on Earth when rejection was already decreed in Heaven? Maybe Apostle York was blessing *and* curse. Maybe this was reprieve dressed up in punishment. He let the river's free flow convince him. He thought of a hundred burdens washing away, the yoke of sinners, the confessions of reckless conscience. Let somebody else worry about mothers sticking blame unto sons and fathers sticking penises into daughters.

Freedom washed over him. He was knee deep in water, splashing, kicking, and twirling, compelled, but not happy. No joy then, but perhaps release. No smile but a gasp. Not a laugh, but a sudden, sharp intake of breath. Bligh removed his pastoral jacket, pulled off his pastoral shirt and undershirt, and stepped out of his pastoral pants and shorts. He closed his eyes and baptized himself.

When Hector rose, the clothes had floated away. Making out the white and blue stripes of his shorts, he chased after them, splashing and stumbling several times. He scraped his toes on harsh rocks. He fell and swallowed cold water but the shorts led him like a piper. Bligh heard a laugh; a demon's and a brother's. *Look at it, the most wasted ding-a-ling in Christendom.* Bligh forgot freedom for shame. The shorts teased him through deep and shallow water, coarse and slippery rocks, weak and mighty currents. They stopped finally on a shelf of grass and mud that shot out from the bank and nearly sealed off the river. Out of breath, he bent down and grabbed them. When he stood up, there in front of him with her arms akimbo and her face scowling was the Widow. He quickly left her face, looking down at the broad shoulders and thick arms that came from years of man labor, the curveless plunge of her black dress that frayed right below her knees.

"Kiss me raas! Look what the man of God come to?"

He let the quiet between them grow thick. In the past, drunkenness would have saved him from embarrassment, but now he had no hope but that she would slip away. And should they pass each other, both would be shrouded in their own tribulations and acknowledge no acquaintance beyond a nod. He remembered who she was. The Widow Greenfield had buried her husband five years before and stopped coming to church since.

"Running bout the river like some mongrel dog with you business hanging all out o door. But then that is nothin new for you. Well, what you have to say for yourself?

"I suppose cock mouth catch cock. Well, me no know what prospect you have down a river so you might as well come with me. Unless God coming back with a three-piece suit."

She stepped off, not looking to see if he would follow. There was nowhere to go but behind her step. He followed her, but not because another night of mosquitoes was unbearable. And not because he would again be under a roof. He followed her because he was now a man stripped of authority and went where authority told him.

As soon as he saw Brillo Road all sense of relief vanished. The two of them walking the entire length of the street (Widow Greenfield's house was near the top) created much fuss. One that showed Pastor Bligh what existed beyond shame. As he hobbled dripping in shorts, each step laid bare new humiliation. The defrocked and disgraced Preacher was on the street from which he had been banished with no liquor to diffuse his awareness. The children laughed. The wives whispered. The men turned away. Only Lucinda could make this worse. Or the man in black. Always the man in black. A force, an apparition, never Apostle York. If that were not enough, there he was walking several paces behind the Widow as if he was a dog or a servant. What existed beyond shame? More shame. Disgrace as deep as grief that eroded dignity in ways that were more dreadful than one could imagine. An embarrassment so thick that it disconnected from the subject, mocking him and leaving him even more ashamed. If only the Lord would kill him right now at this very moment. Before Gibbeah would see him drag his feet into Widow Greenfield's house.

REVIVAL
Part One

Six men, seven women, and three children got saved on Sunday. Most lived outside Gibbeah and would never be seen again, but the number was still more than all the years of Hector Bligh's pastorship, by Lucinda's count.

Just after he prayed for salvation and sent the newly saved to their seats, the Apostle commanded The Five to remain at the altar. There they lingered, one standing alert, one fidgeting, one glancing right, the other left, the last to the floor, all fearing they would be made an example of.

"In the name of the Father I rebuke the evil spirit. I bind it by the blood of the lamb! I loose it from their dreams and thoughts and cast it back into Hell." Then York spoke a language never heard before. All that happened next, happened to Tony Curtis first. Mute since an accident at twelve, he screamed a noise that shook the church. He had not yet fallen when the rest of The Five began to yell, scream, and fall to the ground in spasms. People remembered that before Lillamae stabbed Pastor Bligh she had damaged each of The Five who tried to subdue her. So when Brother Vixton leapt up screaming, *Hallelujah!* his stiff neck was stiff no more. Brother Patrick remained on the floor bawling at having taken his first deep breath in two years. Deacon Pinckney clutched his left eye and cried when he saw out of the right one. Brother Jakes thanked the Lord that he wore tight briefs, as his miracle brought a flush of fear. His blessing stood erect all the way home, where for the first time in two years he could violate his wife.

~~∽~~

"You think it goin dry by itself?" she said, an annoyed parent in the weight of her tongue. She was in the bathroom with Pastor Bligh, losing her patience. After eleven years with a man, she no longer recognized the walls that men and women kept up between each other. To turn away from a man merely because he was undressing or shitting seemed as absurd as lying about the blueness of sky. She certainly wasn't leaving before he handed her the shorts.

This was what she would do to him, he knew it. She would make him young, but only in the most wicked sense of the word. He was to be reduced from man to child, helpless and under manners.

She left him there, closing the door with a man's strength and stirring up a wind that chilled him. Lavender rose up to his nose.

After she became a widow, Mrs. Greenfield restored femininity to the bathroom. The rest of the house still carried the manly stamp of her husband's presence. Rooms with patterned wallpaper that haunted her with tobacco, Old Spice cologne, red dirt, and Earl Grey tea that only he drank. The bathroom was not only pink but lilac and purple, with a translucent shower curtain trimmed with crocheted lace. An oval carpet covered the tiled floor and the lid of the toilet. The mirror, also an oval, mocked him and he looked away.

This must have been where she reclaimed herself. But there was nothing about the Widow that he could color pink, lilac, or purple. Maybe this was where she left behind a former self.

Water hit the back of his neck and he pissed on himself. He had heard of showers but had never felt one before this day. Little rays of water sprung from multiple holes like a hydra and attacked him at once. He raised his arms and let the water wash away secret stenches. Water beat his face, punched his eyelids, and pushed wrinkles away from his cheek. What a thing this was to make him feel young again. This was a chance to be new. God's gift.

Pastor Hector Bligh was fifty-three years old but guilt had pulled down his face. The promise of towering height was thwarted by his slouch. He was on the brink of a new resolve when his thoughts went south. The shower had led him to believe too much. He wondered if people left their homes similarly deluded every morning because of invigorating water jets. His dirtiness could never be washed away. The Widow barged back into the room, unconcerned with his shock or shame.

"No you just bathe in river water?"

"N-no . . . Y-Yes . . . I . . ."

"Suppose you need white soap to feel white as snow. Here me think you did need the holy spirit. Suit you'self. Towel in the closet outside. Anyway, I need the toilet."

"The toi—"

"Me have to pee-pee! You understand me now?"

She pulled down her panty before he went to the door. He left the room clutching his crotch, almost slipping as his wet feet skidded across the floor. Before closing the door he heard her piss stream pierce through the pool of toilet water. The Pastor grabbed a towel from the closet and waited in the hallway. In minutes she emerged, wiping her hands on her skirt.

"Follow me."

She took him down the hallway to the dining room, which had a dim light. From the dining room she swung left and he followed her to a darker bedroom. Although only 2:30 in the afternoon, the room spoke of twilight. Clothes were everywhere, as were chests, cupboards, and books that had not been opened since her husband died. In the center of the room was a four-poster bed. Each post had been carved with a pattern of vine leaves, which twirled and danced to a knob at the top. The Rum Preacher thought of Jack and the beanstalk and an invisible giant suspended right below the ceiling but above the bed.

"You can stay in here."

"This is where—"

"Yes, this is where. Yes. But since him—I don't sleep in here no more. Any more of me business you want to know?"

"No. Tha—"

"Dinner at 5:30. I suppose you can wear him clothes even though him did little shorter than you. I suppose if him have a problem him can always tell you, you bein spiritual and all."

Once alone the room became larger, more blue, more twilight, less him. Bligh remembered again he was fifty-three years old. He had his life all planned out by twenty-two. At forty he would slip into retirement for twenty years, after which would have come obscurity, gardening, and death. Irrelevance was to come after, not before. For a God so ambiguous, there were no two ways about his punishment.

Dinner was to be served at 5:30 p.m. Hector Bligh whispered a prayer that along with the sunlight, memories of the day would lose color and fade into blackness

"The food getting cold."

He sat down. For a woman who seemed to care little, she certainly prepared a table before him. There was simply no way she could have cooked all of this herself. Yet many women in denial of the emptiness that death brought still cooked as if the home was full. This was nothing new. Behind the mask of extravagance was the void cut open by grief. She had fried chicken in batter with honey garlic gravy to the side, steamed rice and peas and sweet potatoes, crushed bananas with butter, and shredded sweet carrots and cabbages together, then sprinkled them with cane vinegar. In the center of the table was a large glass pitcher with red punch beside two plastic cups.

"Help yourself."

He would have rather she helped him. This was an uncomfortable experience, filled with disquiet. He remembered the unease, a child's discomfort as he waited for his father to punish him. In that stiff silence there was nothing but the agony of him guessing. Too much food would be gluttonous. Too little would be scornful. Oh that he could simply eat like a man and be done with it. Women wanted men to be men, after all. Why else would such bounty be laid before him? Why prepare a table in the village of enemies? He piled a mountain on his plate. Food all steaming, dripping, savory, and chunky. His first real meal in years. The Pastor had a woman who cooked, but her meals suffered from an unsavory sameness. Two bites into the Widow's meal, he almost choked on bliss. Juices came alive on a tongue that once felt dead. A million zesty kisses, each more delightful than the one before. The plate was empty and restacked in minutes.

"Mind you choke," she said.

The Widow appeared to smile but then she pushed her chair back into the dark before the Pastor could confirm it. She ate nothing herself. Dinner was a noisy clutter of mouth sounds. Lips and gums slapping food with spit and teeth slicing, tearing, and chomping the whole thing down to paste, followed by the glorious gulp of a swallow.

He was the only one doing the eating, so she must have been doing the watching. Women loved to watch men eat, he thought. It was the last blast of primal energy that the hunter-gatherer had left to show. But whenever he raised his head, even suddenly, hers would be elsewhere, lost in her own inner space. A bitter place, the Pastor concluded, but no more so than his. As she showed no interest in watching him, he decided to watch her. She was a pretty woman, but used her bitterness to look older. The frown between her brows fought against the suppleness of her dark skin. She plaited her hair without care, but had little gray. And there was no diminishing her large, round eyes, no matter how much she scowled and shrunk them. But widowhood came too soon. She was the youngest of them in the village. Old women were better prepared. When intimacy dies, the man dies with it. There will come a time when the bed becomes a gulf and two not-young bodies give up on being one flesh. The chill of sexual heat will be the first death. The silly talk of lovers giving way to instructions, rebuttals, and refusals will be the second. His discovery of a quiet place inside his head or outside the house is the third death. Drinking the fourth. Disease and his mind rotting away, the fifth. Bathing and cleaning him like a child, then combing his hair and scooping away his shit, is the sixth death. And when the seventh death comes—when his lungs collapse, his eyes go white, and the flies know first—the sequence is as banal as dusk.

But Mr. Greenfield died young. She carried the memory like Sisyphus. This was the thing that widows did until death came for them too. God had saved her from seeing her husband's death herself, but the drunkards saw. They said this of his death. He took four shots of rum, cursing his hard-to-please wife with each gulp, then walked in a straight line from barstool to door to road. He stepped into the loud blur of the truck speeding by and vanished, leaving nothing but the echo of metal and glass slamming into flesh.

Within a week the truck was back on the road, picking up stones the villagers broke from rocks. At the funeral, one of the few occasions where Pastor Bligh was sober, the Widow went up to the casket, whispered something, and left the church. She did not return, not to the funeral or the church. Several members of the choir, those who stood near the coffin, swore that she cursed

God that day. Widow Greenfield went home and put curtains over her windows. Marriage was a journey neither she nor her husband had packed for. They had no children.

The Widow looked up and their eyes met. Her face was bland. Not relaxed, but resignatory. He looked down at his empty plate.

"Thank you. Thank you."

"You welcome, Pastor."

"I, I going back to the room. I—"

She waved him off and he felt dismissed and offended. But what he saw when she looked away was a woman who knew nothing more than how to live in a broken space. Had she opened up her brokenness to him? He went back to the room confused.

9:30. There was a theory that he had, which he even preached, that every person in the world had a God-shaped void in his heart, but few chose to fill that void with God. Maybe he filled his with liquor. Or guilt. Whatever, the emptiness gnawed at him. Emptiness was an unnatural state. Frustration or guilt. Is that what a Wednesday night had become, a choice between two unsavory states, with happiness anathema to either? Pastor Hector Bligh wanted a drink. They called him the Rum Preacher, but he never drank rum, preferring whiskey. Scotch had a sulfurous skin, a bitterness that punished you for thinking you had the chest hair to drink it. He thought of this. A room of drunkards, all downing a liquor that nobody could enjoy. Onanism? The bitterness of malt was the bitterness of life itself. But the drink stirred a dumb faith. A stubborn hope that at the bottom of that glass, at the bottom of his life, at the last drop of substance, there must be some final note of sweetness. There had to be. He was beyond reason.

9:45.

"I goin out."

She was still at the table. He wondered if this was where she slept. Maybe she was waiting for her husband's ghost to come for dinner. Maybe this night he would stay away and she would watch the roaches and mice as they pillaged the table. Then they'd gnaw at her flesh and there she would still sit, waiting not out of faith, but because there was nothing else to do. She did not answer.

There was one place to escape God's white throne of judgment. Maybe not so much an escape, but the musty roof, rollicking ska jukebox, and lazy tongues muffled Jehovah's thunder. The bar. Drunkenness was a communal and personal pleasure at once, a miserable state only to those not drinking. Sobriety to him was a cruel attack of conscience masking itself as awareness. If sober people were so aware, how come they only spoke truth when drunk? Give him the romance of a drunkard over the indignation of a teetotaler any day. At the door of the bar, the clink of glasses, the haze of smoke, and cheerful talk of sin welcomed him.

"The mistress is here?" Bligh asked.

"No baba."

"She sick?"

"Why you want to know, you goin heal her?"

He looked at her, this little girl trying on a woman's tongue for size. There was a fate for girls like her. It started with a smile and ended with several ugly children and a husband who would beat her for her rudeness.

"You said she sick?"

"Me never say nothing to you."

He did not even know the girl. She aged before him into a woman older than what Widow Greenfield was trying to be.

"She staying home. Say she reading her Bible," the girl finally said.

"Bible?"

"You turn echo now that you done be preacher? Yes sah, she on fire for Jesus ever since Apostle York kick—I mean, come take you spot. She into the Bible reading hard. She all a talking bout selling the bar. Poor people soon out o work." She looked at him as if he was responsible. The Pastor said nothing. She had wanted him to say something. She was ready. The girl had an unbroken stream of expletive prepared that would have withered him where he stood. But he fed her nothing and she stood there with the stillborn response stuck in her throat, too nasty to swallow.

"What you want?"

"Scotch and soda water. The mistress, she always forget where she keep the soda."

"But it right underneath the counter."

"No. What I meant was . . . she always forget where she keep the soda."

"You ears hard? Me say it under—"

"Is a game between me and she, just pass the soda!"

"You mean Scotch?"

"Yes, Scotch! Scotch! Scotch!"

"Hey, don't jump after me cause bigger-balls man go make you look like bitch."

"Leave the bottle."

Let the Rum Preacher testify to this. He was far more comfortable at the bar than at the altar. As the head of the church he could never escape the collective weight of judgment. But that cup had passed, and sliding toward him was another, wet, golden, and tinkling with ice. What lay beyond shame, freedom? He was seven sips away from not giving a damn, fifteen from not remembering who he was, and twenty from pissing on himself. *Take it easy, Preacher,* the bartender would have said by now, but she was off enjoying company more divine than his. With her absent, there was no one to talk to but himself. He was drunk. This was usually a state of perfect peace, but something had gone wrong. Usually, whiskey could erase a sentence midway before it was even finished. Like chalk on a blackboard, the memory was never gone, only smudged, indecipherable and irrelevant. But this time memory came in waves, history he had forgotten for years. Suddenly, afflictions not his own were thrust upon him. His left eye went black. A pain ran along the course of his spine and he fell off the barstool. He tried, in a desperate fit of wheezing, to catch his breath. A force unseen hit him in the scrotum, a battering ram, a rolling calf. The Pastor doubled over, lost his balance, and fell on the floor. Whiskey and bile erupted from his stomach. His teeth chattered violently, chomping on his tongue and causing his throat to fill with blood. He threw himself into the fit, as if a spirit was trying to flee his body. Bligh's eyes rolled back into his skull and his head hammered onto the floor.

"Jeezus Christ! Him have fits! Him have fits!" said a man beside Bligh as he fell.

"Rahtid," said another.

"Unu fling this spoon in him mouth quick!" shouted the young bartender. "Bout him want bottle! You know say is a whole o Johnny Walker him one go fi drink?"

"Him still a fits?"

"Is the Devil in him. Me read that in the Bible," said the man nearest to Bligh, holding onto the spoon that he had shoved in the Pastor's mouth.

"If you read Bible, me frig with donkey," came from the end of the bar.

"Me no business a wha," said the bartender, "Get him out o the place!"

"Me? Me nah touch that deh, baba. You no see that him still having fits? You want him kick one o we?"

"Whoever take him out get the next three drink free," she said.

"Like is your bar!"

"See it deh! Him stop jerk now. Alright . . . alright . . . alright . . . There. See, him stop shake. Now give me me spoon and get this shithouse out of me bar. Mr. Cee, you and him drag this damn Rum Preacher out!"

"Little girl, you giving plenty order to man who don't work for you."

"No, me ordering whichever man want him next three shot of rum for free."

"Drag him go where?"

"Outside, down the road, straight to Hell, I don't care. Just take him out o—Jezuss Chrise! Is what so stink? Don't tell me say the man shit up himself! Take him out! Take him out!"

They dumped him at the gate of Widow Greenfield just as dawn sneaked in under night's empty cover. The Widow had waited. She grabbed him by the left foot and dragged him into the house. The Widow undressed him clinically, but it would have disturbed him had he been conscious. She was matronly, even aloof. Men were children anyway, only taller.

He had no real sense of what she had done until a day later when he awoke on the dead man's bed. In the darkness of the room they came— flashes and memories like still shots robbed of context by scattershot recollection. His head bumping across the tiles of the bathroom floor. His shirt being pulled away in one violent swoop. His feet in the air as his pants were pulled off. Him falling to a loud splash in cold water. A quick flash; the Widow rubbing her nose. A roll, a tumble, and a splash in the lilac bathtub. Lavender and soap. Wet cloth on his face, his back, his feet, and scooping between his buttocks. A hazy female. A blurred face. A hand (his?) reaching for her breasts and squeezing out of wonder, like a child. A palm striking him like black lightning. Lavender water. His chest heaving and choking, his back bouncing off blows from her hand as she forced the water out.

She pulled the Pastor out of the tub and dried him with pink towels that smelt of soap.

WILDERNESS

Bligh woke up to see the sun cast a white glow. Never before had the room been so full of light. The walls that before spoke of evening now spoke of the vast expanse of noonday sky; the lightness of floating or being. The dead wood of the bed seemed to come alive and the carved vines grew real leaves, flowering instead of disappearing at the top. But the light carried no heat or warmth, only the sterility of electric light. Or Heaven's light.

He had finally done it. He had finally drunk himself to death.

Every man had his own image of Heaven, shaped not by what was read or heard, but feared. His picture, loose vignettes of castles and streets and gowns and teeth all colored white, was not shaped by a dream of Heaven, but a nightmare of Hell drawn by Dante and Jehovah's Witnesses pamphlets. The nightmare followed Bligh from childhood to manhood undiminished by his growth or knowledge. To him, Hell was not just a lake of fire and blood. Hell was a place where good lives and good intentions were burnt away, robbed forever of purpose or fulfillment. Guilt, on the other hand, was left to roam free and torment. This brought about a sense of ease that even he knew was perverse: If this was Hell then damnation was something he had already lived through. But this was something else.

He knew she would appear, and she did.

Hector. These are the things that must happen to you, whispered a voice that was strange and familiar.

She looked exactly as he expected her to. A child, cherub, fairy tale, or perhaps an old evil. A strange and familiar face. White skin, light brown hair that cascaded to narrow shoulders, and eyes with no pupils. She said nothing, he said nothing, they both knew. These were the things that must happen.

Her hair stirred even though there was no wind. He saw through her eyes to a second face and a millionth; she conjured every man and none in one blink. The girl laughed. An experienced Madonna and a divine child. She went toward him, pursing her lips as if to kiss, but from those lips she blew a hurricane. Dust whipped itself up in a torrent of screams and his world went black.

He woke up without breath. Sleeping on his back, his own spit had choked him. Bligh punched himself in the chest, hacked, and coughed. He rolled over to the side of the bed to spit, but more than spit came. Vomit splattered the floor. His chest heaved with each spasm, punishing him with agony. His legs remained on the bed while the rest of him sunk to the floor. There was a stench and sweetness to the vomit that made him want to vomit more. His chest heaved again, but nothing came.

"Nice, just fantastic."

The Widow had come in the room to see only his legs on the bed. She grabbed him by the ankles and pulled.

"Where you rolling to, Timbuktu?"

She smelt the vomit and frowned, covering her nose.

"Shithouse. Tell me is not . . . Oh shithouse! You mother never teach you how fi use bathroom sink?"

"I'm sorr . . . I'm sorr . . ."

"Everybody raasclaat sorry, but is not everybody have to clean up people mess. Your God coming soon? Cause if him coming right now I giving him a damn mop! Look at this shit."

"I'm sorr . . ."

"I'm sorry too. Sorry I let some friggin drunkard back in me house to vomit it up. Maybe I should give thanks and praises that things never come through you other hole. I goin for the bucket. Try not to vomit til I come back."

Bligh wiped his mouth. His face was wet from sweat.

Hector. These are the things that must happen to you.

Hector jumped. The voice sounded like a little girl and a man at the same time. God's voice? He knew the sound but forgot the face. The Widow came back with a bucket and a mop. She cleaned the floor in silence as Bligh lay still in the bed, looking at the ceiling and feeling the weight of his guilt and his hangover.

These are the things that must happen to you.

* * *

Evening.

"The bathroom is right through there if you don't remember," the Widow said and left. "You hungry?" she shouted from outside his room.

"No," he replied in a whisper. He was out of breath and perspiring dreadfully. The wetness alarmed him at first, but that went as he drifted into a stupor again. The bed became waves pushing him back and forth. He reached out to grab the bedpost but his hand trembled so wildly that he missed.

"Me say if you hungry?

"Pastor?

"Pastor?

"Shit."

He had fallen off the bed again. She thought he had passed out, but as she grabbed his shirt to pull him up, he grabbed her hand. His head rolled back and forth as he tried to hold her gaze. "Leave me alone," he said.

"You sickly. What I going do is—"

"Leave me alone! You, you can't help me. Leave me alone."

"Suit yourself," she said with as much apathy as she could fake, and released him. The Widow swung the door shut and threw the room in complete darkness.

"Jesus," he said.

The Pastor lost track of day and night. There was only darkness and heat. In the room of the dead man he heard nothing but the Widow's shouts, which sounded like fake echoes from some other wilderness. He had never been this sick before. Usually the depth of his nausea could tell him how long it had been since his last drink. But this was different. Hector could not distinguish past from present or dream from real. He heard his brother cry in Heaven, *Why did you betray me?*

Bligh staggered out of bed and went over to the room's sole window. Outside, the sky had the grayness of dusk, but he did not trust what he saw. His hands trembled in both dream and truth, so he gave up on telling one from the other. Wetness ran down his face, armpits, back, and down his legs. He made one step away from the window and almost slid in his puddle. Bligh couldn't remember when he pissed on himself.

At first he thought demons had attacked him in sleep, but then Bligh realized that he had not slept at all. These were the dreams of the awake, torments of the Devil. He would do anything for a drink, but he could hear his voice inside his body saying no. Was that how God's voice sounded now? Like his own, but with an authority he had never heard before? Maybe the Apostle was blessing *and* curse. Maybe Bligh deserved both. He fell on his knees but couldn't pray. From the window he watched the moon as she mocked him.

He knelt for what seemed like an hour, but he could not really tell. Outside looked like late dusk or early nightfall. He glanced up at the wood planks in the ceiling and something flicked out of view like a tiny whip.

Or a tail.

He looked up again and saw the shadows of their scurry. Coming up and down, left and right, were rats, rats. Rats on the ceiling that jumped down on the floor.

Hector jumped over them, stepping on one and crushing his squeal. He leapt on the bed and pulled his knees up to his chest, feeling the coldness of his pissed-up pants. Rats loved decay. In the blink of an eye, they covered the bed.

"Jesus Christ! What the raasclaat you screaming bout?"

The Widow had rushed into the room again, expecting the sudden smell of fresh puke. He could see the rats clearly, but could not make out the Widow's face, only the sharpness of her tongue.

"All around me . . . all around me."

"What? What you saying?"

"Them all around me! All around me."

"What is all around you? Demon? Where? Then plead the blood, you no preacher?"

He jumped and she jumped as well. Her fear was as real as his, even as she tried to cuss her way through it. Hector pulled himself up with the bedpost, swatting rats away from his feet. He stared at the bed, so she looked as well, at the manic folds in the white sheet and the dampness of sweat. At nothing. Then she saw his face.

"Oh, Jesus."

"All around me! All around . . ."

She could think of nothing else. The Widow ran out of the room as he began to scream about rats. The Pastor kicked them away from his toes and they would pull back like a wave only to roll in with more. The Widow came back with a glass, climbed on the bed, and grabbed him by the shoulder.

"Pastor, get ahold of you damn self!"

"Rats, rats, rats, rats, rats, rats, rats, rats, rats—"

"Pastor!" Authority cut through illusion. The rats were gone.

"You not seeing no friggin rat! Drink this and cure yourself." She forced the cup between his lips before he could say no.

Bligh spat the rum out and coughed. "You trying to kill me?" he shouted.

"I trying to save you, you ungrateful sum'bitch! This is the only thing that can save you."

"That's what—" he could barely catch his breath. "That's what killing me."

"Maybe is the only thing that keeping you. Me know man like you, you know. After a while you stop breathe air that don't have no liquor stench on it. After a while it's all you can do, even if it—"

"Killing me. You want it to kill me like it did your husband?"

"What?" she said in a bare whisper. "What?" she asked again, even though she knew she couldn't bear him saying it twice.

"Nothing. Nothing. I said nothing. Please, go. Leave me alone."

She left him.

"Mrs. Greenfield?"

"What?"

Bligh pulled the blanket up to his neck and spoke without looking at her. "You have a key for this door?"

"What you think?"

"Then lock the door. Please. Lock the door."

"You must lick your head. You can't even piss by yourself and now you want—"

"Please. I'm begging you. Lock the door. And don't open it no matter what you hear. Please. I'm begging you. Please."

"Suit yourself, cause you mad as shad. But don't shit up me sheet." She slammed the door, leaving Bligh to feel the thickness of darkness.

Not long after he heard the click of the key, his penis grew hard. At the foot of the bed, with her face hidden in wild black hair, was his brother's wife. She was only a ghost now, with vapor rising from her skin. His brother's wife was naked and white. She straddled him and he unzipped his pants. Hector closed his eyes and felt the room's heat between his legs. But when he opened them he saw that she had no face, only a skull and a few teeth. Bligh screamed and the wife disappeared.

"Jesus!" he shouted. "Jesus! Jesus!"

The Widow obeyed the Pastor's request for a day and a half. She had tried not to care, to not even pass his door, but her heart betrayed her. Mere concern, she told herself; after all, she was not made of stone. Mere concern, no different from what she had for the feeble or the elderly or the wounded or the wretched. Mere concern, she said to herself.

On the evening of the second day, she let herself in the room. The rankness of piss surrounded her. The bed was empty. Under the window, the Pastor snored.

"Oi, Preacher man.

"Pastor.

"Hector!"

Bligh woke up. He pushed himself up by the elbows until sitting on the floor, with his back to the window. The Widow watched him. He knew she had something to say.

"I know what happen to you," she said, and closed her eyes for several seconds before opening them again. The Widow looked at him directly. "God leave you."

REVIVAL
Part Two

Women, unevenly split between wife and spinster, old and young, prepubescent and menopausal, filled the front pew. They were caught up in the way he sweated even though three fans spun above. The way he pounded into the podium: two tiny taps followed by a resounding thump whenever he said, "Cut it out! Cut it out! Cut it out!" Maybe it was the coolie blood coursing through him that made his hair seem always wet. Unruly. Moreso, they were caught up in his dance. When the Apostle gave a word, a sweet word, chased by a blast of organ and a chorus of Amens, he would jump and spread his arms wide, shouting, *Hallelujah!* Sweat would fly from his fingers and kiss the women in the front row who felt blessed indeed. Yet the Apostle seduced men also.

The third Sunday, halfway into praise and worship, the church was shocked into silence. Fourteen feet, unfamiliar to holy floors, stepped nervously into church. The Apostle waved his hand and the organist quickly recovered from his pause as the choir jumped back into the chorus. The Rude Boys, the bad boys of Brillo Road, had come to church. Ungainly and in front was their leader who was dressed in his yellow T-shirt and camouflage green pants. He removed his cap and wooly locks sprung like flowers. Red bobby socks disappeared inside his shock of a shoe. The Apostle was waiting. He stretched his hand and pointed to the empty left side of the second row.

That Sunday, the Apostle York spoke about the Front End of the Call:

And it came to pass, that as he was come nigh unto Jericho, a certain blind man sat by the wayside begging:

And hearing a multitude pass by, he asked what it meant. And they told him, that He of Nazareth passeth by. And he cried, saying, Thou, Son of David, have mercy on me.

And the Son of Man stood, and commanded him to be brought unto Him: and he was come near, He asked him,

Saying, what wilt thou that I shall do unto thee? And he said, Lord, that I may receive my sight.

And the son of man said unto him, receive thy sight: Thy faith hath saved thee.

And immediately he received his sight, and followed Him, glorifying God: and all the people, when they saw it, gave praise unto God.

Lucinda had seen too much forty-five minutes earlier. Her eyes were so wide open they burnt her to tears. From that day, she would never see anything in quite the same way, but the sermon was not to be blamed.

"Beloved, when Je— Oh praise God! When the Lord, the mighty God of Heaven and Earth, forgives you. I'm just going to read something from Matthew, Chapter Four, verse eighteen to twenty-five."

Fifteen minutes before the hour, Lucinda had been stocking hymnals behind the church benches. She was feline in her purpose. The woman never wore perfume, but her new freshness and bounce had brought heat and sweat, and the need to pound her chest with Cussons talcum powder until it looked like a breast of bird feathers. She now took baths with lavender floor cleaner, which she poured into the bath water, ignoring the burn in both holes. A trivial thing to do, but Lucinda had fallen in love with the trivial and now played with the petty. She would tell him the hymnals were carefully stacked, just to make sure he knew that she was responsible. She wanted his approval, even if that only meant the slight rise of his left eyebrow and the tentative curl of his lips into a smile. She was surprised at how much she wanted to be wanted. Lucinda's life had been so efficiently clipped and blinkered that she had desired nothing from a man but distance.

"Apostle, the hymnals put out pon the bench. You want me do the Bibl—"

The keys slipped out of her fingers and fell to the ground. She had cracked the door open slightly. Inside the office, on the floor, were red books and black books, opened and unopened and scattered throughout. The Apostle stood firmly, almost facing her, with his hands on his hips. But he was looking behind him at the full-length mirror. He was naked. Her tiny gasp cut through the din like thunder. He swung around and saw the blur of her as she closed the door and ran off.

For the first time, Lucinda sat to the rear of the church, staring at the floor as the sermon passed by in a blur.

. . . Going on from there, he saw two other brothers, James, son of Zebedee, and his brother John. He called them and immediately they left the boat and their father and followed Him.

"Beloved, when the Lord opens your eyes, because how many of you know that we're all blind? And if we not blind, some of us can only look behind us. But church, when the Lord opens your eyes it's your invitation to follow!

"Listen to me.

"Now is the time to follow! Any time the Lord reveals something to you, He wants you to be like Elisha. Sell off everything! Get rid of everything! Join Him now, church. Don't waste any more time in that woman bed you should not be sleeping in. Or spending that money you stole, or reading that letter that you should not be opening, or gossiping that lady you shouldn't be gossiping, or drinking that liquor you shouldn't be—oh, do I have a witness in here this morning? Don't let me start preaching, church! Cut it out! Cut it out! Cut it out!

"The Lord is looking for followers. Remember the story of the rich man in Mark Ten? Or Eleven, don't look it up. You know why we don't have thirteen disciples? It's not because Adam and Eve sin on Friday the thirteenth. You know why we don't have thirteen disciples? Because the last one couldn't throw down everything and follow the Son of Man. Now he's condemned, still burning in the chambers of fire, mind you, and all his millions of dollars can't buy one snow cone in Hell. Is that where you're heading?

"He's calling you.

"There are things you need to burn. Destroy. Give up. Leave behind. If this is you, meet me at the altar right now, praise God!"

The altar was full. A man screamed *Jesus!* and collapsed. The Apostle stepped over him to get to the others. Lucinda remained at the back, trying and failing to sweep her mind empty. *Holy Ghost. Holy Ghost. Holy Ghost. Holy Ghost. No foreskin. Holy Ghost. Holy Ghost. Holy Ghost.*

"Lucinda."

His voice pulled her from the cluster of thoughts and she realized that the church was empty, save for the man still lying on the floor whom she did not see. Lucinda spun around; shocked and embarrassed that time had passed and left her with him. She could have carried herself out in the wave of those who left during altar call, even though not many did these days. Instead she was alone with him. He sat one pew ahead with his back to her and his unruly hair glistening like a thousand tiny eyes.

"Lucinda, I think we need to clear a certain matter up. What you might have *thought* you saw."

"Y—yes, Pas—I mean, Apos . . ." She stared at the floor.

"Lucinda? Lucinda," he said for a second time, disappointed with her unease. "Lucinda, pastors change their clothes in the office all the time. I know what it might have looked like, but it was all innocent, trust me. You might find it foolish, even funny. Here it is: I was changing clothes in my office and there I was, just as how God made me, and you know God, he's no respecter of persons. I mean, come now, how many times has the Holy Spirit given you a revelation on the toilet? Nothing wrong with that, God is God. Anyway, there I was, about to put my clothes on, when BAM! God just give me a word so powerful that I nearly wet myself. Well, I had to drop to my knees and give Him ten Hallelujahs on the spot! Like I said in today's message, when God opens you eyes, He wants you to do it now! You hearing me, Lucinda? You can never keep God waiting."

"Yes, Apostle."

"So I drop to my knees thanking God, and it was then, right when I got back on my feet, that you saw me. That is that." He turned around and faced her. "I'm so sorry."

"Yes sah."

"You forgive me?"

"Apostle?"

"Forgive. It's an old custom. Usually happens after somebody says they're sorry."

"Yes sah."

"You don't look forgiving."

"Apostle?"

"Forgiving look. You know, with a smile. What is it going to take to get a smile out of you? Are you ticklish? Maybe I should call down one of God's angels to tickle you?"

She laughed a little girl's laugh.

"Aha! Look at that. Nothing like a smile to wake up a beautiful face. This means we're still friends. Good. And Lucinda, I promise I'll leave my changing to the bathroom from now on."

Before she was thirteen, Lucinda's mother had beaten her in two. She gave the two halves names, Day Lucinda and Night Lucinda. Her mother was the same, a church-going sister on some days, a spell-casting obeah woman and whore on others. In time the woman came undone, and to survive her, or at least to prevent whipping, Lucinda would split in two to placate her mother. There was Day Lucinda, when her mother felt pious, who spoke about Sunday school and friends she did not have. There was Night Lucinda, who helped her mother find the callaloo plant; not the one everybody ate, but the special callaloo to make tea for fellowshipping with darkness. When her mother would beat her savagely, which was often, Day Lucinda would hide bruises under a demure calico dress and a taut heart. When her mother lost her way, which was often, Night Lucinda would steal her cat's teeth, lizard skins, beads, and knotted cords and speak to the Sasa in secret. Lucinda carried her two selves into adulthood with ease, using both to empower herself over other women. But then came the Apostle.

Day was for discipline; night, chaos. Day was for white gloves and skirts below the knee, night was for goat blood on black skin. Day was for stiff lips and Bible verse; night was for an orgy of one with a green banana as her incubus. Then came the Apostle and she saw Jesus in his face, but a serpent below his belt. There, in his crotch that bulged when he sat down, legs uncrossed as they always were, to show her the shift key on the typewriter. Two Lucindas collided at the junction of his crucifix, nesting in hairy skin, pointing to the bold red tip of his circumcision. She could no longer tell day from night.

So Lucinda whipped herself to sleep. Jesuits did this in Kingston, she had heard from a church sister. She imagined seven priests all in a row, whipping their bloody backs while staring at their hardened penises. They would whip until blood flowed like tributaries and their erections shrank in shame. She deserved no less for being a whore in the way she thinketh. Lucinda had known the Apostle just as surely as Ham had known his father Noah in the Bible. She became both at once. A drunken Noah, staggering naked in his tent, knocking over food and drink and crashing on cushions, spread wide for nature to see. She could see a body hardened by obedience, giving nothing to age, pissing and farting with that magnificence that men had when they did not care. Lucinda blinked and became Ham, his dark son, who slipped in the tent and was blinded by magnificence as well. She became father and son at once, shuddering through drunken blindness at the father's sudden pleasure, shaking with fear and sin as the son took his father in his mouth. Lust came to her when most unwelcome and shattered the wall she had constructed between her two selves. It was the damn blood. That cursed time of the month that played out in wetness, pain, and bloat; that stirred a frenzy deep inside her pinker self. Twice in her thoughts he had made her burn bright with his own flame, as red as his books. Jesuits did this. She wanted to be good. No more Night Lucinda. She would whip darkness out in the name of Jesus. In the closet it waited; the black snake, the belt reserved for disobedient Sunday school children. She took her blouse off and stared at her weakness in the mirror, at her breasts, one drooped slightly lower than the other. She saw his wings, the demon of her sin waiting to rip her legs open. Consuming fire. She pleaded the blood of Jesus and swung the belt over her left shoulder. The leather tore through soft skin like a massa's whip. Lucinda shook, tears fell, and she looked at herself again. Now for resolve. She beat out the Lucinda that could not serve the Apostle with purity, swinging the belt over the right shoulder, then left, then right, then left, then right again. And again and again and again until there was nothing but leather slicing through the air pungent with flesh and blood. The mirror spoke her shame in a chant until there was nothing left between her and it but light.

Dressed in two shirts and torn cloths wrapped up, down, and crossway over her back, Lucinda went to church. That she had appointed herself secretary was neither questioned nor challenged. Her first duty was to dispose of the multitude of cakes that came daily from every widow, spinster, and daughter who had reached consenting age. *It was good that a man not marry.* That's what the Bible said. Even better for an Apostle. There was no need for the distraction of a wife; all he needed in a woman he had in . . . She trembled, yearning and fearing the end of her own thought. The office needed cleaning. She began by putting his red books on the shelf.

"Lucinda?"

"AAAH!"

"You reach here before me? I starting to wonder about you, you know. Maybe you're coveting my job. I didn't startle you, did I?"

"No! No, Pastor, I mean, Apostle."

"I'm pulling your leg, Lucinda. But still . . ." He went over to his desk. "We have to do something about that constant slip of yours."

"Slip? It a show?"

"Excuse me?"

"Me never mean to sin with this short frock."

"Slip of the tongue, child."

"Oh! Me did know that, Pastor, I mean, Apostle."

"See, I caught you again. There you go, calling me Pastor. Do you miss Pastor Bligh?"

"No baba! Me miss him like me miss seven plague of Egypt in me panty. Lawks, sorry, Apostle."

He waved her off.

"Him is a abomination before the Lord. Him is—" she started.

"Still a child of God and God loves him as much as he loves you. God gave you permission to rebuke him?"

"Jes—" He covered her mouth quickly. She smelt the soap on his fingers and did not think it strange. When he let go she could taste his salt on her lips.

"Y—I—we—ye—"

"Wasn't exactly a shining moment, y'know, Lucinda. Driving a man of

God out of the church. That was one cup that I prayed would pass. Look at me. Even a fallen man of God is still a man of God, y'know, Lucinda. He's still my brother. If we were all so perfect why would we need the Son of God? Lucinda, maybe Bligh needs Him more now than ever and instead of driving him out we should be greeting him with a holy kiss. I mean, doesn't Second Corinthians say that after we expel the immoral brother we must welcome him back or risk the Devil's will be done?"

"I don't, I don't understand."

"Shhh. Don't work your head about it too much. The Lord has forgiven me and as His faithful servant, I have forgiven Pastor Bligh. You know where he is?"

"Yes, Apostle."

"Send him a message for me. Tell him that Apostle York says that he can come back."

SCHISM

By five o'clock, fat amber clouds had shaded trees orange, a shock before nightfall. Dampness and drip gave the weekday the stamp of Sunday. Evening rain made a day forget herself, but never her purpose. Rain did the same for people, frightening them to cover or freeing them to expose, but never allowing them to forget their purpose. This damn blasted rain was holding her back. And yet this could not wait until tomorrow. Nothing he said could ever wait. Lucinda was to tell the Widow Greenfield that the Pastor would be allowed back into church, but only to worship. She must be told tonight. Delay was disease. The only cure for procrastination was purpose. She covered her head with newspaper and ran down to the end of Brillo Road.

As she came up to the crossroads, Lucinda saw the Widow's house, its sole front window flickering with dim light. But as she stepped and splashed in the road's center, a multitude of black wings, a hundred or a thousand, burst out in a thunderous flutter. She was blind in the darkness, but when the wings flapped, the air shook. Demon-sized crows. Man-sized demons. They shrieked and spun with the wind. Lucinda screamed and heard her voice vanish in the vortex. She would be sucked up in the swirling darkness. Lucinda shut her eyes tight and hummed a hymn. She opened them slowly to see them gone and the rain weakened to a drizzle. She ran to the house.

"Mrs. Greenfield? Mrs. Greenfield?" She listened for a flutter. Her last knock swung through empty space. The Widow had opened the door. "Mrs. Greenfield."

"Kiss me raas. What *you* doin here?"

"Mrs. Greenfield, I—"

"You goin stay outside and get wet up or you comin inside?"

"Me never did plan to, but—"

"Suit yourself."

"Mrs. Greenfield—"

"Make me ask you something," the Widow interrupted in that tone the Rum Preacher knew. "You see any Mr. Greenfield here?"

"Well . . . ah . . . no."

"Then why the backfoot you calling me Mrs. Greenfield? You forget say me know you long time? Long before you get high and mighty like God love you special."

"Our Father love everybody special."

"Yes, but everybody know Him have a real special love for you."

"Anyway, me never come here fi talk bout me."

"Eehi? Then what you come for? Come make we go lap frock tail and labrish, cause me no know what you could want from the Widow woman."

"Is not me why him dead, y'know."

For nearly a minute the Widow stood at her doorway, starched and beaten. Lucinda's eyes swept the ground as she listened for a sudden flutter. The Widow's hands trembled. She felt them coming, memories banished years ago of her husband's crushed face hidden in a closed casket. Memories that came back because of this bitch, her enemy ever since adolescence gave the Widow bigger breasts and beefier buttocks. The Widow came into an even greater hatred of her, something renewed for the day.

"At least him don't have to hide from *you* no more. Climb any ackee tree since mornin, Lucinda Queenie?"

In obeah-man country there are several teas. People think the secret history of witchcraft is of oils, but that is no secret. Oils are given to those who pay, but tea is for those who believe. There is cerasse to ease the stomach, soursop leaf for nerves, and comfrey for health and strength. But there is another tea with a name lost to those who live in light. A tea that is prepared in hidden places that nobody drinks alone. Lucinda's mother hid the secret callaloo under her bed and never gave her daughter that warning. Lucinda had mixed the tea as her mother had done, boiling the weeds and gulping the acrid broth down in three, then covering her mouth as it scalded her gut. She filled her mouth with river water and spat into the fire. A huge cloud of steam rose and surrounded her in mist. Lucinda felt cold, very cold. A wet wind stirred and hissed. She was no longer on the ground or in clothes. In a blink she soared so high that Gibbeah became a dot of flickering light. In another blink there was nothing but moon and sky. She screamed and laughed. Lucinda willed herself there and suddenly she was. Nothing would stop her revenge. From up in the ackee tree she saw them. The bride and groom, years from becoming Widow and corpse, consummating their marriage. In the moonlit glimmer of the bedroom she saw the manic movement of sweaty flesh. The whiteness of the Widow's feet, up in the air and bobbing as her husband fucked her. Each thrust cut through Lucinda's blackened heart. Mrs. Greenfield came and opened her eyes expecting to see love all wet and real. But instead she saw a shadow falling out of the ackee tree. The shadow's hair was parted at the middle; the way Lucinda kept it until the day of her death.

Lucinda's hands were shaking as she stood at the Widow's door. She turned to leave but the rain was waiting and she feared the beat of wings. Did the Widow hear the flutter? Her face was unchanged.

"Tell him that the Apostle say him can come back." Lucinda turned away. The rain swallowed her up and she was gone.

The Rum Preacher had heard. Widow Greenfield stood in the doorway looking out, but was aware of the clumsiness of his stealth.

"Look like you church want you back." As she turned, he looked away.

"You think them goin kill the fattest calf?"

She was in the mood. Lucinda had whet her appetite for more. No damn way she was going to be miserable by herself. The Preacher withered, slipped back into his room, and left her to the dead space. The Lord giveth and the Lord taketh away. He prayed in thanksgiving.

Rain fell all night. Some wondered if God had turned back on his promise to never flood the Earth no matter how much man sinned on it. Rain fell on the righteous and unrighteous. Rain fell on Clarence when he left Mr. Johnson's house after fucking Mr. Johnson's wife, as he did most nights while the husband slept soundly in the same bed. Thunder judged him and he left her in a flurry. Clarence was a good distance from the house when semen wetted his thighs, reminding him that he had forgotten his briefs. Then lightning struck, exposing him in a flash of light, and he forgot again. Clarence ran home, stumbling twice in the muddy water.

Lightning was the pointed finger of God's judgment. The people of Gibbeah knew this well. Lightning had killed the Contraptionist. Its blinding light exposed iniquity, its singular force burst through the dark skin of sin. The Contraptionist was a lonely man who lived not in Gibbeah but less than a mile beyond the river. Each day he was seen twice: driving his cows to the field at dawn and back to the pen at dusk. But from his house came the sound of industry. The bustle of hands and machines and hammers and saws and pulleys and ropes and wood at work.

One evening, just before the rains came, a curious odor drifted from his shed, something sickly and sweet. As quick as the wind, the pleasant smell of something cooked gave way to the horrific odor of someone burnt. When they found him, the rain had begun in a rhythmless drizzle, but thunder bellowed and gales came upon the village in swells. He was around the back of the house. The contraption looked like a guillotine: two towering planks of wood on both sides of a narrow platform, which was encircled by a fence. Pulleys at the top of the planks suspended ropes downwards. Each rope had a harness to which he was strapped at the thigh. This was his breakthrough invention; now he could adjust his height to fuck cows of any size. From afar it seemed as if women's garters were pulling him up. When the lightning struck he had already mounted himself, supported by pulleys and excited by the friction of her buttocks. The sudden blast of white light and heat had burnt him to a crust, singeing the rope and planks of wood and fusing the pulleys stiff. The cow was unharmed. For two days, nobody approached him and he swung in the wind with the burnt rope squeaking as it rubbed against the wood. Even in death, his deeds were exposed. The lightning had struck him when he was most ready, and now, more than his exposed parts would remain stiff forever. The men took him down after Mrs. Fracas's dog made away with all the toes on his left foot. Lightning was the pointed finger of God's judgment.

The Rum Preacher had been praying without stop from before dawn. He heard the rain break. The Widow was right. But didn't the scriptures say that only by blaspheming the Holy Spirit would the Lord leave you? He was an abomination. The most wretched sinner there was. Before, he knelt, but now he fell to the ground grieving for himself.

"Thirty years. Him blood flowing for thirty years. Oh Jesus! Jesus! Jesus! Holy Spirit! Precious Lord! Forgive me! Holy Spirit! Holy Spirit! Take pity on You wicked son!"

His brother fell over the balcony again. Blood spread across the floor unevenly, looking like a map. Hector had coveted, lied, and stolen from his brother. Then he destroyed him. Back in the dark bedroom, Bligh rolled on the ground and sobbed. His cries grew louder, waking the Widow, who crept up to the door. What she saw took her back to a place when she was a woman. She looked at the man and saw a child, maybe a lamb. Her hardened heart broke and she left him.

"Father, give me the cup. Father, not my will but Thine be done! Please, Jesus. I ask for the pain. I ask for the death. I asking for the crucifixion. I want to rise, Jesus, I want to rise. I want to rise!"

Not once in those years since the seminary had he asked for forgiveness. Not once had he felt worthy. Even now he begrudged his brother's life. His brother's joy. Fearlessness. Silliness. He hated his brother's life of choice, where his was one of duty. Bligh could still see himself mounted atop the sister-in-law, his penis the hardened point of his envy. In mere hours he corrupted her, made her lose faith in love and give herself to him, a man becoming a priest. Or so he lied. Honesty rose to the surface as before. She had called him to bed. She had no faith in love to gain or lose. Like Adam, he was led by his serpent and her apple; to break his virginity only to fall into the horrible knowledge of good and evil. After his brother died she disappeared.

But with the Apostle came Hector's turn to feel the loss of everything. God's justice. He loved the Lord but hated Him too. These were the things that must happen, a girl said to him in a dream. But other things stirred in him, things that would never have risen had he not been brought down so low. He never thought much of his life when he had it, but things were different now that he had lost everything. This must be new. Having been driven from the church now made him want the church back. Those whom God loved, God punished, and God had never punished him until now. For thirty years he thought himself no more than a blind spot on God's backside, dreading yet needing His mighty hand. This was what drove him to drink. How wrong he'd been.

Hector Bligh, as it is in Heaven so it is on Earth, how long must this be about thee?

How long must you be your own God? In happiness and in sadness you are still the Lord of your world. It was never whether you were forgiven. The Moon spins around the Earth, the Earth spins around the Sun, the Sun spins around the center of the Universe. And yet none has more significance than a speck, a dot, an ism, no more, no less. How much less are you to the Universe? And yet look at the image in which you were made. What a piece of work are you! Forgiveness happened on the cross, so what right have you to feel the anguish of the major prophets? You ask for life but my gift to you will be blindness.

Images came with no order or purpose. Children. Darkness. Wings. Black walls that screamed their witness. Crosses swinging from sweaty chests. A withdrawal. The warm spurt of semen. Screams, howls, a wave of purple and white. A face; a brother, a lover, a mirror that falls and shatters. A Judas on the ground, a Jesus swinging from a noose. A little boy bent over. With hair so alive and serpentine locks. Boys blended into girls. Seraphim, cherubim, infant. He knew them. Not their faces, but their sizes, the blackness of their hair and the lightness of their skin. From the dark came a man whose black robes blended with nightfall. He had the height of a man and the face of a child. His robes stirred even though there was no wind. As Bligh rose from the floor, he knew who the man was and why he came.

Apostle York.

Pastor Bligh dressed himself in the suit that the Widow had found down by the river and brought back to white. He opened the door to the scent of eggs and frying bacon.

"Is where you going?"

"To the church. That man who calls himself Apostle."

"You no think that foolish?"

"God used foolish to confound wise."

"Don't preach to me. The egg getting cold."

"I don't have time to lose. God goin do a wor—"

"Either way, you have to eat, so God goin just have to damn well wait."

"But I—"

"Look. Don't make me get stink with you. Egg and bacon not cheap, so you either eat it or me goin throw hot oil straight on you white suit. Think say people get up early to cook breakfast and . . ." The rest she said with her back to him, but the Pastor was already struck. It was better to say nothing.

"Eat up. Something tell me say today you goin need to be strong. Real strong."

Lucinda was early to work. She knew what she wanted to see, yet told herself that she had no such desire. The memory of whipping made her back burn anew, yet the suffering was imaginary and failed to deny or suppress. She looked through the keyhole and saw black. Surely he was already at work. Lucinda chastised herself. What was she there to see anyway, crouched like a nasty child at the door of her Apostle's office? She looked through the keyhole again and saw black. But then the black moved and her heart jumped. Black became shadow. Shadow became curve, curve became buttock. The buttock went right and disappeared from view. She shifted right and struck her temple on the doorknob. Ignoring the throb of pain, Lucinda stood by the keyhole for several minutes until she resigned herself to disappointment. She rose and walked straight into his chest.

"Oh Jes—"

He grabbed her by the throat, held on firmly but did not squeeze. She recoiled but the move failed in his grip. The Apostle's eyes opened wide like a child one instant, a judge the next. Lucinda felt her fear threatening to sprinkle down her legs. He held her still by the throat for several seconds and released her, trailing her chin with his fingers. As his index finger touched her lips, he whispered, "Shhhh. Shall we call the Lord's name in vain? Lucinda, what are you on about?"

"Y . . . yuh . . . yuh . . ."

"Did you drop something?"

"Yuh . . . yuh . . . yuh . . ."

"Or maybe you're just sleepwalking? Which one is it?"

"Ugh . . . I . . . bathroom!"

"Well, dear, don't let me stop you."

Lucinda rushed to the bathroom where she willed herself to vomit. Her back's burn was real.

"Lucinda?"

She jumped. Fear was making her sick. At first he sounded so intimate that she thought he must be inside the room. But the voice came from behind the door.

"Lucinda, are you okay?"

"Y-yes, Past—I mean, Apostle."

"Feeling sick?"

"NO—Yes. Sick in some part of me body, sah."

"Oh my, I'm sorry to hear that. But, praise God, better to have a sick body than a sick mind, eh?"

"Yes, Apostle."

When he walked away, a presence or a memory came to her, she was not sure which. She recalled a little girl's body exploding and blood scattering across rocks. She recalled a man and a woman mixing sweat under the cover of ackee leaves. She recalled the smell of the pit toilet and the sound of children, six or sixty, laughing. Lucinda grabbed her belly and retched.

Sunday jumped to Sunday fast. But the Rum Preacher was ready. On Wednesday he had run to the peak of the hill with no shoes. His heart pumped hard and burst from the solemn shell of three decades. On Thursday he read the Book of Psalms from beginning to end on his knees without break. On Friday he sat beside Daniel in a pit of lions, and on Saturday Jesus retold the Sermon on the Mount for his ears only. Greater than he had faced less, but the Lord had appointed him. Besides, God said that victory came not by power or might.

The Widow watched all this with cynical bemusement. That was her defense against faith, but still he sparked something in her as well. She did not know what that was, but was sure that she did not want it. The Widow grappled with too many unwelcome things, including more than a little concern for Pastor Hector Bligh.

"After all Him do to you, you still a pray to Him. You is the biggest fool in Gibbeah."

"The Lord giveth and the Lord taketh—"

"Away. God must be a Indian giver."

He stepped away from her, but she followed. Her tongue was loose.

"Me just want to know why. Tell the Widow woman why you still down on you knee after all this. You think God can help you? God couldn't even help Him damn self down cross, how Him fi help one loser like you?"

"Is not God do this to me. Is me do this to me!"

"Then God allow it, or Him couldn't do nothing bout it. Me no understand how you can love anybody with them friggery ways."

"Because God is God."

"And shit is shit."

"Because God is God."

"I know who your God is. Him right there in me kitchen cupboard, marked 80 proof. God is a Devil."

"What the Hell you want, woman? You think the Almighty is Father Christmas? God is El Shaddai. Him don't owe you nothing. The Lord giveth and the Lord taketh away!"

"Me know you not talking bout me husband. Me damn well know you not talking bout me husband."

He stepped away, but she followed. He walked faster, deeper into the house, not looking ahead but hearing her stomp behind.

"Where the bloodclaat you think you a go? Me talkin to you bout you God! Come evangelize to me, no? Come evangelize me."

He was surrounded by doors, all closed save one. She was right behind him and her voice pushed him into the room. It smelt of carbolic soap, of cleanliness brought by disinfection and purging. There were seven crucifixes on the wall, all made of wood and all turned upside down. The bed faced the wall and had no sheet or covers, only a striped mattress. The wind slipped through shut, louvered windows and whispered the truth of this room to him. The mirror was turned to face the wall, as were the two paintings and the dresser. Near the door was a print of Jesus, the same that hung on church walls and grocery shops, with his head tilted as if curious, with light bouncing off gentle brown hair and with eyes wet and glimmery below eyebrows raised for pity.

The picture was slashed up, down, and crossway and the heart, surrounded by a crown of thorns, was cut out. God had left this place. He knew.

"Yes, look. Look! Look good. Is that Jesus me pray to now. Jesus that no got no heart. Jesus that no got no soul. My Jesus good fi Him word. Look!"

"Oh Father who art in Heaven . . ."

"Hallowed be His goddamn name."

He was cornered, she was wounded.

"God didn't put the rum glass in his hand."

"Who is you to talk, you is a bigger drunkard them him ever was, but you still living."

The Pastor said nothing.

"God never want me have him so Him take him away," she continued. "Not that you same one love say? God giveth and taketh away. Why you take him away, eeh? Why you take him away?"

"Miss Greenfield—"

"Why you take him away? You have million and million and all me have is one, and you take him away."

"Mrs. Greenfield—"

"You know what me want?"

"No, Mrs.—"

"You know what me want, Jesus?"

"Mary . . ."

"Me don't want to be no widow no more. Me don't want be no widow. Me want to be a woman. You can give me that, Jesus? Give it to me, Jesus, give it to me, Jesus. Turn me back into woman. Give it to me, Jesus." She had lifted up her skirt and there were no panties underneath. She moved toward him, her eyes wet with tears and fingers gripping the swept-up skirt tightly. Between her legs was dark, empty. "You can turn me back to a woman? You can turn me back to a woman, Jesus?"

"Mary Greenfield!"

"Me have faith, Puppa Jesus. Me know if me touch it, it will heal me." She grabbed his crotch and squeezed. Hector pushed her off, harder than he intended. The Widow stumbled onto the bed, sobbing.

"God not giving him back, Mary."

He was afraid to step past her. A mission waited outside the door but the

Devil had blocked him in. In his spirit her chest was pushing against his, her hand grabbing his penis softly one second, harder the next. This was the Devil's work and he was no respecter of persons, not even a broken Widow woman. There was nothing to do but stand, his white suit drawing light from the darkness.

She curled up in shadow, sniffing, wiping her nose and looking down on the ground. "Get out," she said.

Now that Sunday mornings had thrown off lethargy for entertainment, the energy was electric. The faithful were here, as were the amused, the riveted, the bitter, and the curious, some not from Gibbeah. Apostle York saw the crowd gather from his window. He sat still with a fire in his eyes. The beard hid the healed sore below his lip, but there were others above and below his belt. They reminded him of what had come and gone and what had not yet come to pass. He knew worse would happen soon, but this was not a morning to dwell on what crept beneath his skin. Lucinda had left the day's notices on his desk and he saw two little spots of red peeping from her back. York touched his lips with his index finger, silencing his spirit. The organ sounded and raised the first chorus. He reached for his black and red gown.

They swarmed the front rows like penny stinkers. The rest of the faithful filled out the middle rows, leaving everybody else to the back benches.

Today he was to speak of many things. He was ready. He told the congregation to turn to the Book of Mark, Chapter Four, verse three.

Hearken! Behold, there went out a sower to sow: And it came to pass, as he sowed, some fell by the wayside, and the fowls of the air came and devoured it up. And some fell on stony ground.

There was a commotion outside. The impact hit the church in waves, from outside to in. The Apostle was hit by reverberation. At the front of the church he would be the last to catch the news.

"DISGRACE!" said the voice. Firm, with an authority that nobody had heard from him before. Pastor Bligh stood gleaming at the foot of the church's steps. His left hand held an open Bible and his right pointed to the steeple. The few who had come to church when he was Pastor were astonished to hear the man shout, yet there he was, bellowing like a risen spirit.

Inside, the Apostle did not know what was taking place. "Church, settle down. Let's not have any distractions.

And some fell on stony ground, where it had not much Earth; and immediately—

"ABOMINATION!"

The Apostle heard a war cry. Anger was an emotion he cursed. Bemusement was better, amusement was better than that.

"Looks like somebody escape from Bellevue in God's good morning. Now what is the world coming to, church? Let's get back to the scripture and let the Lord have mercy on that poor soul.

And immediately it sprang up, because it had no depth of Earth: But when the sun was up, it—

"ANTICHRIST!"

The Apostle's own three words had returned to curse him. The book fell from his hand.

"Who the Hell is that?"

Rumor would spread that his eyes went red. Lucinda was already ahead of him, and she returned, hopping and skipping like an imp with a secret.

"Is Pastor Bligh! Is Pastor Bligh!"

Hector Bligh held his ground as the sun baked his back. He felt what he thought was youth, but was the disappearance of twenty-two years of burden. People had a way of carrying afflictions like possessions, thinking suffering was the evidence of life. But the Holy Spirit had made him new. It had revitalized his moribund body with purpose and promise. Maybe he was overextending like Icarus, but his hand felt greater than the wind and mightier than the sun. He would stand in the middle of the road and not be moved. They came out to meet him, Lucinda first, followed by The Five, Clarence, and finally, the Apostle York.

"Well, you too ugly to be any woman's son so what should we call you? The Prodigal Bastard?" the Apostle said.

"I can think of a couple names for you," returned Bligh.

"Really now. But look at you, eh? Maybe I should have my congregation's arse's flogged. I mean, look at what it did for you."

"I know your ways. I know you."

"You don't say. Couple days ago you didn't even know yourself. But let me remind you, because you've gone from drunk to deluded. You, Hector Bligh, are a stupid old man. You're a failure, you're a drunkard, and you're the mess that never turned into a message. Now you're rising up like you were dead for three days, but do mankind a favor, Bligh. Do Gibbeah a favor. Stay down. You hear me? Stay down on the ground. It's the only place you're fit for. Just go back where you came from and have a good sleep. Speaking of sleeping, how is the Widow? Does she have you under heavy manners?"

The crowd laughed in uneven rhythm. Some had never felt tension so tight.

"Bligh. Bligh, stop embarrassing yourself. Stop embarrassing the God you serve. He forgives you. I forgive you. In good time Gibbeah will forgive you. And you know what? I'm sure somewhere deep down in Hell even your brother forgives you. Did he trip, did something he saw push him over, who can tell these days?"

No sound came from the crowd.

"God was there, Bligh. God was there the day your brother died. It must have felt really—what's the word I'm looking for? What, what, what. Noooo, not that one, no that's too . . . no . . . I know! I know the word you would use. Heavenly. *Le petit mort.* The little death. Must be something for a man to see his preacher brother mounting his wife like a dog bucking a bitch. You see this man?" York shouted. He was circling Bligh as he spoke. "Everybody in Kingston knows this man! Everybody know the destruction this man unleash from his pants! Everybody know about you and the in-law!"

"She wasn't a bitch . . . th, th, that have nothing to do with this."

"But it has everything to do with this, you uncouth negro."

The Apostle continued to circle the Pastor as he spoke, but then stopped right in front of him. Close enough for Bligh to see the scar below the Apostle's lip.

"You think that because your clothes are washed clean suddenly your soul is white as snow? You think purity comes from washing soap? Why don't we all do it like you, Hector? Here we are sanctifying ourselves before the Lord, covering ourselves in the blood of the lamb, when all we needed to do was take a bath. But I believe your story, you know, Bligh. I think he just tripped. Ever hear a neck break, Bligh? You think there would be a crunch because of bone, but it's almost like when you snap a carrot.

"Thwock!"

The crowd jumped. The Apostle's face was less than a foot from the Rum Preacher. He whispered.

"But I'm sure he forgives you. I'm sure the woman would write a letter to you right now, if she could get two sentences out without crapping herself. Did you know she was in Bellevue? Stop making a spectacle of yourself. Please. I could let this town know all about you, but you know what? Even I believe in redemption, Bligh, and you're an old man. Show some dignity and stop embarrassing God." The Apostle York turned his back to him and walked to the church. Mid-stride he turned around, smirking.

"Besides," he shouted, "I'm sure we can find some way to occupy you in church! Maybe a broom to sweep the floor. You're already doing it with your arse." The man in black walked away while the man in white held his ground.

Lucinda followed behind the Apostle quickly, stopping once to glare at Bligh.

"*Ye are of your father, the Devil, and the lusts of your father ye will do,*" spoke the Rum Preacher.

The man in black stopped.

"*He was a murderer from the beginning and abode not in truth, because there is no truth in him.*"

"Bligh."

"*When he speaketh a lie, he speaketh his own: for he is a liar and the father of lies.*"

"Hector Bligh, by all that's Holy."

"Not a damn thing bout you Holy, but I know you."

"I serve the way and the truth and the light," countered the Apostle.

"Your light blacker than black. I know you."

"You know me? What do you think you know? Half of your mind you already burn away with liquor. You who throw your dung on God's altar. Backward Kingston boy lost in country, what do you think you know?"

"I know bout your red books and your black books. And I know why you come here."

"Rhetoric, rhetoric, so much rhetoric. Tell me, does God have His hand up your arse? You being a dummy, I figured, but God a ventriloquist? This is new. You're mad, Bligh. Such a sad development. There was a time when people smiled when they spoke of you. Now they laugh."

"Then let them laugh. Who laugh last, laugh best. Soon there will be wailing and gnashing of teeth. But I will deal with you first."

"Deal with me? You know who I am? You—"

"I know who you come for."

"Bligh. Don't come near this church again or I'll—"

"Ephesians Two, verse twenty. Ephesians Three, verse five."

"Bligh."

"Second Peter One, verse twelve to fifteen."

"I swear I will . . ."

"Jes—"

The Pastor hit the ground before the Apostle felt the spit and blood on his own knuckles. He raised his hand to punch Bligh again but stopped suddenly and turned away laughing. He laughed all the way back into church and closed the doors. They swung open and he grabbed them quickly, forcing them shut.

777

It was soon coming Easter.

The Apostle tell we to chop down plenty coconut leaf, cause the next Sunday is Palm Sunday. Him goin make the pickneys put on show right in the church! We no see so much excitement since Miss Fracas dog give birth to cat. Anyway, it was soon coming Easter.

Everywhere did lay down with coconut leaf. From the pulpit, right down the aisle, all the way out the door, down the step, and out the road. Some of we who never used go to church now go every Sunday cause you know you goin see signs and wonders! We see man who couldn't talk, talk, and man who couldn't walk, walk. Is Jesus Christ Himself who send the Apostle to Gibbeah.

The Apostle tell we to sit down. But that is lie, him never tell we. All him do is look at we and we know. That is how the Apostle good! Him know we before we know we! When him want people to do something, him just look pon them a certain way and them do it quick. Anyway, we sit down and the old man who play organ start play. Then Lucinda get up and run to the door. She waving her hand and telling somebody to come inside.

Coo pon the show! As soon as she step aside, the first two come in wearing pretty purple cloth, the expensive one that the shop have to order and take three week to come. Then two more little pickney come in. Them have candle in them hand and sheet over them head that tie round the forehead. Them look like little angel. Two more come in and still two more, a girl and a boy. You should a see what come next! A big boy come in the church pulling something behind him with rope. Him pull and pull, him even cuss pon the quiet, but the rope don't budge. Then him make one almighty pull and lo and behold, is donkey him pulling into the church! People start clapping like clapping goin out of style. And who fi deh pon the donkey, but the nicest, sweetest, prettiest, beautifullest little boy. We did think that only Mr. Garvey nephews did so cute with nice skin and pretty hair, until we see say is wig the boy was wearing. A long brown wig on him head and cotton balls pon him chin fi make him look like Jesus. Talk bout excitement!

All of them line up at front of the church and start to sing My Cup Is a Running Over. The Apostle wave to the choir and everybody start singing too, but the little Jesus was the loudest voice. Is was the sweetest thing! So sweet that we never hear him right away, but then little by little some of we notice that one sound wasn't goin along with the music. Is then another wave start roll over the church. This wave did tell you say something did wrong and was getting wronger. In no time all church did quiet cept for the little Jesus who nobody did tell fi shut up. Soon is was just the two of them, the Jesus boy singing My Cup Is a Running Over at the front and the Rum Preacher screaming bout the pit of Hellfire and damnation at the back. Him come in when everybody was looking at the pickneys, so nobody see him. Now him standing in the middle of the church aisle and pointing to the pulpit.

And Jesus asked him, saying, What is thy name? And he said, Legion, for we are many!

Those of we who did in front see the Apostle face go from pretty to ugly. Him scream out like the roaring lion and look straight at Pastor Bligh. Apostle York head turn red, like pig that choke and dead. Him vex! Him point at the choir and they start sing real loud. The whole o we turning head from left to right, cause one minute the choir a swoop up the chorus, then the next minute the Rum Preacher a burn up the back.

We perplex. After all, everybody did know Bligh when him did fenke-fenke, but here him look strappin, like David with a slingshot. And him loud! This couldn't be the same man who pee-pee himself and make demon girl beat him down. Is couldn't him. This man who we seeing now, nobody could a drive him out o him own church. But there him be. Even people who know say the Apostle come from holy Jesus Christ Himself start listen to the Preacher.

The Rum Preacher talkin bout woe this and woe that and woe to the man through who they come, but seeing him was enough. In him white jacket and white shirt and white pants. The sun sneak in and him blast open with light. Then all that white surround with black. Apostle York command The Five to grab the Rum Preacher. One grab him right hand and one grab him left shoulder. The Rum Preacher kick out but them catch him two foot and drag him out o the church. All the time, the Rum Preacher shouting and scream-ing and Hellfiring bout a man who need deliverance and who writing demon doctrine. Some say is accident, some say them do it on purpose. But all five of them crash into the wall near the doorway and the Rum Preacher head slam into it like battering ram. The Preacher quiet after that.

Outside, the Preacher in the middle of the road and him didn't move. Him white suit did cover all over with black. Him roll over and try to get up, but crouch down low. Inside, the Apostle talkin bout how him disobey God Himself by inviting that abomination back into the church when First Cor-inthians clearly say we must expel the immoral brother. The Apostle say that God already pass judgment pon the drunken bastard and is our duty to leave God work to God and hand the man over to the Devil.

"Beloved," said the Apostle, "turn with me to Exodus Chapter Twenty:

> *Honor your father and your mother so that your days will be long in the land the Lord is giving you.* Say that with me again. *Honor your father and your mother so that your days will be long in the land the Lord is giving you.*

The Apostle closed his book and grasped the podium with both hands. "Who is a father?

"Come. Let's check the scriptures deeply. King Saul, a terrible king, yes, but how bad a father could he be if he raised Jonathan? Now we have King David. Everybody loves King David but lo and behold, as Mrs. Fracas would say, his own son tried to kill him. How about Samuel, who spent so much time prophesying over people's sons that he couldn't even see his own sons growing into liars, thieves, and perverts. How about Joseph, father to the Son of God and he didn't even notice his son was missing until three days later.

"Here is the truth. You don't need a father or a mother. Let me say this again. You don't need a father or a mother. All you need is the Heavenly Father. And another thing. I don't want anybody to call the Lord's name in this church. Oh, you're quiet now. Let me say it again. I don't want anybody to call the Lord's name in this church. Who can tell me why? Why would I forbid calling the name under which all demons tremble? Well, let me ask you a question . . . Vixton, what is your father's name?"

Vixton, along with the rest of The Five, was already standing.

"Adolphus, Apostle."

"Tell me, Vixton, what do you call him?"

"Nothing that me can say in church, Apostle."

Some laughed until they saw the Apostle's face. "There's a season for laughter and that season is not today. Vixton, seriously, what do you call your father?"

"Well . . . ah . . . Papa or Mr. Dixon or P when his ear take him and him can't hear much."

"Why not Adolphus?"

"Because . . ."

"Because he is the head and not the tail, the ruler, not the follower. Because he is the father, you show him due respect. Due respect. So tell me something, Vixton. If you show your earthly father so much respect, how much more should you show your Heavenly Father? Calling God by his first name like you and Him is size. Listen to me, cut it out! Cut it out! Cut it out! Until you can show me, until you can show God that you are more than babes in Christ, I want everybody to address the Father as the Father. He is not your son, or your friend, or your lover. He is your master, and me? I'm just like you. I am His serv—"

Before he could finish, singing disrupted church. The Rum Preacher was outside in the exact spot where he had been beaten and dumped the Sunday previous, singing "Rock of Ages." His voice was thunderous, full of blood and melancholy. The Apostle heard his song and felt the hatred of Cain for the Preacher, newly able. York pointed at the choir, who erupted into "God Is a Good God." The chorus rose above the song of the Rum Preacher and consumed it. But as soon as the choir's song sputtered to a close, there was Hector Bligh, his voice rising. A few in the church began humming with him. The Apostle pushed away the podium in a rage and it fell, sending books skidding across the floor. Nobody dared speak. York pushed open the church doors.

Outside, the Preacher and the Apostle were face to face, separated by yards, years, and ever-mounting animosity. The Rum Preacher kept on singing, his notes rising and falling with the hymn. He looked younger. He seemed to have a new strength, and nobody knew where it came from, though some thought the bed of the Widow Greenfield. The Apostle had no time for Lucinda's rumors. He turned away from the Preacher but stood in the doorway. Those who had turned to look turned back.

Hector Bligh stood firm. But gray spots blotted out his sunlight, moving left, right, and in circles. He looked up and saw a mass swirling of black that broke away when the John Crows scattered. "Rock of Ages" led to "Onward Christian Soldiers." Three of the birds landed and met the Pastor with a gaze. Bligh sung. The first flapped his wings and took off, then the second and the third. They rose to a low height, no higher than the steeple of the church, then folded their wings and dove straight for the Pastor. Bligh clutched his heart, closed his eyes, and kept on singing.

The Apostle, his back to the road, folded both arms behind him and rubbed his knuckles. The Pastor's voice had vanished amidst the scream of vultures. When the Apostle turned around his jaw fell so far that he grabbed his chin to prevent spit escaping. The Pastor was on his knees, in the middle of Hanover Road, with his eyes closed but his arms wide open. Before him, behind him, around him, all the way up to the church steps and down Hanover Road, were dead vultures. John Crows with necks broken, heads crushed, and wings ripped away. The Pastor was praying in a circle of untouched road as the sky drizzled black feathers and blood.

Things done change. Some people feel it, some people know it, but nobody see it. Is one month now. We know that Pastor Bligh bring shame pon the land and is God judgment that drive him out of the village. Last week service everybody on fire for the Lord. Praising and singing and shouting and clapping and even those dutty Rude Boys get baptize! But then the old preacher come back. None of we know how, cause him was so fool-fool before. Him step up the road with purpose like him is John the Baptist himself. Them say is Widow Greenfield to blame. Them decide to do something bout her.

This new preacher. Some people don't trust nobody who look too pretty. Lucifer was the son of the morning. Nobody see what the Apostle do, and who him do it to nah tell. And that was just Thursday gone. Widow Greenfield should a look behind her.

She round the back washing clothes. The Widow scrub so hard that she never see them sneak up. By the time she look all of The Five surround her. One of them say something and she start cuss loud. Then all of a sudden she grab one of the clothes that she washing and swing after them. Them jump out of the way and Brother Jakes grab her and push her down on the ground. Then Brother Vixton, he step on her breast and cuss her. This time all sort of noise start come from inside the house. A thump, then a bump, and then a crash and a splat one after the other. Them turn her house upside down while Brother Vixton crush the Widow chest. The rest of them come outside. Them just shrug them shoulder. Then Brother Vixton stoop down and say something to the Widow and laugh. Widow Greenfield spit in him face. Brother Vixton still laughing when him stand back up and wipe it off. Him still laughing when him kick her in the belly. She bawl and curl up and Brother Vixton spit on her and them leave. But not before the other one, the one them call Tony Curtis, the one who couldn't talk then but can talk little now, turn over her wash pan and all the water flood the backyard with the clothes sailing over the grass. Widow Greenfield in the dirt crying to herself.

May and October rained the most. Nobody told this to September, who snatched the pregnant clouds for herself. Rain fell on evil, rain fell on good, rain fell on church but kept none away on Good Friday. Lucinda and her flower circle of spinsters, widows, and neglected wives had decorated the church in purple. The Apostle had chosen Luke's version of the crucifixion because it was the most Greek. Lucinda could not understand why he would consider one part of the Bible better than any other, but concluded that wisdom is as wisdom does.

It was the sixth hour
And darkness came over the whole land
Until the ninth hour for the sun stopped shining
And the curtain of the temple was torn in two
He called out in a loud voice,
Father into your hands I commit my spirit
When he said this, he breathed his last.

"Now turn to Ch—"

The scream came from the back, from one of the few not sharing in the Apostle's good news. She left her seat and ran to the back door, where she screamed again. The Rum Preacher was coming up Hanover Road. His feet were bare and the rain had soaked his white shirt and pants, which clung to him, forming a network of veins. Others joined the screaming girl. The Rum Preacher continued in measured steps, his back bent slightly under the weight of the huge wooden cross that he pulled like Jesus. It was cut from a young tree. He braced the burden by his shoulders and steadied it with his arms. Between rain and tears, his eyes seemed to burn.

Good Christian people want to know why anybody would pull up chair next to the Rum Preacher. So people ask people who know people who can ask people and that people, a man, say him don't business bout no chastisement from none of we and we could eat shit for all him care. Man is a man, and must make up him own mind, him say. Man no flaky like how woman flaky; them see one pretty boy and them brain turn to pudding, him say.

People think it funny that little by little more man and woman goin out to hear the Rum Preacher. Him wasn't preaching to none of them really. Him preach to the road and the sky and to God. Another one of them that leave, a woman, say that when he talk to her is like him talking right through her. People say that there is no way the Apostle goin give Hector Bligh the church back no matter how white him suit look these days. But them who gone outside say him don't want the church back. We perplex. Where else people goin find God if them don't have church?

Gibbeah change. And time come for everybody to pick a side. This old man, who was fool to people one time, make sense now. Soon, two more join them outside. People who know people who know people who is the cousin twice removed of one of them, say that she out in the sun because church just don't feel right no more. But everybody else think it feel right so that mean it right to them. See here, the Apostle tell the pickneys in Sunday school that if anything happen to them, they must tell their spiritual father first, who is he.

And him tell people other things. First him saying that Jesus used to walk with money and that if the Devil come to steal, kill, and destroy, we must steal, kill, and destroy back. And how we not to say Jesus name in church no more. And how we need to explore deeply what was really goin on between David and Jonathan. People who know people who know one of the men who gone outside say that the man decide to leave when him hear them things. Him didn't like them things the Apostle was saying. That did sound like some queer business. Some pervert business. Him say the final straw was when the Apostle get into Onan and say that him sin was not backing him fist, but wasting him seed. The man never like that at all. Him say a man must feel shame if he ever back him fist. The man leave and go outside cause him no understand why man would want to jerk him own cocky and go blind when all around you see pretty girl who pum-pum tight. The Apostle shaking up things too much, him say, and the people just take what him say without even a grumble. We make him go. Him not washed in the true blood of the lamb. Many are called but few are chosen.

The Apostle on fire. Him tell the church that to heal the sick we have to exterminate the sickness. Nobody know what exterminate mean, but we sure it mean bringing down Hellfire and damnation. Him saying new things and old things too fast for some people. Them don't know if him talking to God or the Devil, so they go outside too.

The Apostle warn bout this thing that hit Kingston like the Plague in Egypt in Bible Chapter Exodus. Some call it television and some call it TV. Is a box that show picture. The box not bigger than a banana box, but the evil! Him say it right to name the thing TV, cause TV stand for Totally Vile! Or Terrible Vice! Or Trash and Violence! Him say nobody in Gibbeah should ever buy a TV cause it soon go out of style and people goin back to redifusion. Him say that even radio allow straightway for demons, and one day soon and very soon God's holy purging fire will consume the movie theater.

Him say God's people must lean on God's people and Gibbeah should watch who we let in from now on, cause the Devil people can take human form and demons are already among us.

Some people can't deal with this so them gone outside to hear Pastor tell them bout the good news that God anoint him to tell the poor. People who know people who ask people heard from people that Bligh telling his little congregation what them need to hear even if it's not what them want. Them say that if Hector Bligh can stand this Hellfire sun to talk bout righteousness, then they can stand it too.

It came to pass when nobody could remember what happened to the Majestic Cinema. From the start, the story was fraught with an incomplete ending, an unsolved mystery. While the who's and why's were often discussed, answers were tentative and the truth was never forthcoming. This much was known, even though not much was repeated. The Apostle York had said that God's holy fire would consume the cinema and consume it did, even though not many were convinced of the fire's divine source. After all, the Majestic was several miles away. That the proprietor was burnt to ash raised doubts. That two sneaky children from a neighboring village were also burnt to ash raised more. "The Lord was merciful, but also vengeful," the Apostle said. His justice was swift and terrible to those who disobeyed Him and caused His people to sin.

That Sunday, the Apostle York recited eight woes of which the last was the first.

"Woe to the world because of the things that cause people to sin! Such things must come, but woe to the man through whom they come! Don't be foolish, church. You know who this scripture is speaking about. He torments us even today. God is looking for people who will stand up in faith. God is looking for people who will carry out His command no matter how Holy, no matter how brutal, no matter how violent they may be. Who's ready to be violent for the Lord?

"If your hand causes you to sin, cut it off and throw it away. If your eye causes you to sin, gouge it out. Church, right now we have a problem. A problem of two heads, and one head is causing us to sin. He's already lured three of you out into the wide road that leads to damnation. Beloved! A body with two heads is not twice as intelligent. He's a monster! An aberration. The other head isn't a head, it's an abscess! The Lord says cut it out! Cut it out! Cut it out! Come now, church, who is ready to be violent for the Lord?"

Is the Sunday after Easter Sunday and the Apostle dealing with we hard. We no feel this fair. Things did hard enough searching the hymnal for hymn that don't say Jesus. Now the Apostle say we not to have nothing to do with the things of this world cause everything is permit for the Devil. Some people start mumble. But the Apostle don't say nothing that didn't come out of God mouth first. Me not goin to be in the way when God come back to judge the quick and the dead. From me is little girl, the Bible say don't cross with God cause Him would expose we and then Him would punish we. Plenty girl in Hell now feeling fire all the way up to them pokie cause them cross God. God knock down the wall of Jericho and kill every little boy baby in Egypt. God make river stink with blood and Him send Him own people to Babylon fi suffer hard. God kill all of Job pickney and fling Joseph in prison. Is six people outside now a listen to Pastor Bligh and God goin burn them up with Holy fire, just like him burn down the Majestic. You just watch and see.

Hector Bligh think him on fire for the Lord; him just a blaze up the street. Sun did hot but him extra hot. We no know what goin happen to church if anybody else start blaze. But the Apostle a deal with we hard. Him ask we question that nobody can answer. Him ask if we truly ready to follow God, cause all Jamaican people have is mouth. Him ask we again if we really, really, really ready to follow God, cause Christianity is not no play-play religion. Him say to follow God we have to move with God and you can't move with God if you staying where you be. This is why God can't bless Gibbeah. This is why there is a plague on the village and evil rising to flourish. The Devil restaking him claim on Gibbeah but we must resist and stand up for God. Then him get harder, a fling scripture give we like cat o nine pon field negro backside.

"He who has ears, let him hear! If anyone comes to me and does not hate his father and mother, his wife and children, his brothers and sisters, yes, even his own life, he cannot be my disciple. In the same way, any of you who does not give up everything he has cannot be my disciple. He who has ears, let him hear."

Him say that is a special word for Gibbeah's people of God. The word could be for one person or it could be for the whole church. Some of we have to get rid of the thing keeping we down so that we can fly high for God. We have to get rid of sin. The skirts that getting short and shorter. Them Little Richard and Tennessee Ernie Ford and Elvis records, even Peace in the Valley. The ganja, the friend who don't come to church. The drinking, the fornication, the tobacco; we have to give up everything. Even husband have to give up wife, and mother give up pickney, cause them is the things that we turn into idol the most. Anything that have nothing to do with God have nothing to do with we and we must hate them things. We must hate anybody who don't worship God the way we worship God, in spirit and truth every day and night. We must hate anybody who don't see say that when God come to Earth Him was a man who did hard-up and hot and feel the burden of temptation just like we. Anything that God don't have nothing to do with, we must hate it. Anybody who don't come to church, we must hate like poison, that is what God say somewhere in the Bible. It don't matter if is we own mother. The Apostle say that God say that Gibbeah must cut itself off from the sin that so easily entangle. That's what him say. Him say we need to throw down everything and pick up the cross. Him say we need to hate father and mother and pastor who call themself father. Pastor who out in the street and right now dragging a precious few straight down to Hell. "We need to cut it out, church; we need to cut it out! Cut it out! Cut it out! We can't serve God and the Devil," the Apostle say.

After the Apostle done, we did want to kill the sinner man and sinner woman so bad that we did have to count to ten and then again. The Apostle a deal with we hard, but is so truth hard. Plus, nobody believe that after all this time scoring point for the Devil that Pastor Bligh all of a sudden on fire for Je . . . the Lord. This is the man that drunk from the day after him come. Imagine, Preacher gone to rum bar fi chummy-chummy up with drunkard and whore. This is the man who the Devil use Lillamae Perkins to turn into fool, she who drown herself. Him make all man shame that them is man. Plus, when him go fi baptize Mrs. Smithfield daughter, him nearly drown her. All them things we did think funny one time, but is that bastard make God leave Gibbeah. Is Apostle York who drive him out like how God drive evilness out of the temple. The Apostle a deal with we hard, but it better than the Pastor not dealing with we at all. Now him out o street a preach holy fire, but you no need much to do the Devil work. The Devil will take care of the Rum Preacher, so we must cut him off.

People already getting rid of the redifusion, and throwing way the short-wave radio. Anybody who not washed in the blood of the lamb we not talking to. Is time to be strong and upright. Is time to make sacrifice and we know who fi sacrifice first. Apostle York not fraid fi tell we hard things, that's why we believe what him say. All we know say is that Deacon Pinckney could only see through one eye before the Apostle come to the village and now him can see through two. The Rum Preacher never bring one single miracle to Gibbeah. Him bring in the Devil fi take up seat like we and him is combolo. That's why we glad bout what happen to him. We like how God use the Apostle to deal with Pastor Bligh case. Listen, when God use him man, God use him man!

The Apostle in church with the Pastor outside. The Apostle stretch out him hand and start say tongues, but this was no Abba babba tongues, is tongues we never hear yet. Outside, one of them scream and people run to the window to see the six of them scatter from him like ants. People say him was talking bout Jonah and Nineveh when all of a sudden him start bawl out, *Jesus! Jesus!* and start swing him hand like mad man. Me hear say him two eye go white and him start flap round like him blind. Then him knee buckle and him drop pon the road hard. We stay from up in the church and hear him head buck the road. Then him start shake-shake real hard and foam come out of him mouth. Then the foam turn to red. The Apostle stop speaking in tongue and the choir start to sing Bringing in the Shield We Shall Come Rejoicing. The Pastor still on the ground but him stop shake. Him white suit dirty. And him eye still white. Some of we couldn't watch no more, cause we did glad, but we did sad too and that feel strange. Plus, we did fraid o God. We see what happen to people who take him name make poppy show. But we shall come rejoicing bringing in the shield. Little later, Mrs. Fracas say she look back one last time and just catch her in the corner of her eye. Widow Greenfield grab Hector Bligh by him two hand and drag him away.

ROLLING CALF
Part One

Three days after Sunday, she was found, etherized in the blackened river mud, body stiff with rigor mortis. On her back with her legs spread wide, she looked ready for sexual intercourse. She seemed to have drowned. A dead calf was nothing new to Gibbeah, or to Mrs. Fracas, who fainted at the sight. There was no sign of what contributed to the cow's demise except one: Her head was upside down. And though there was mud all over her, there was none on the calf's neck. No cut, no scar, no stitch either. Neck grew into upside-down head as if the animal were born that way. To Mrs. Fracas, who saw the calf first, and Clarence, who saw it after, the answer was immediate and obvious. This was the Devil's work.

The Widow Greenfield, with her grocery list in tow, had a simple mission. She had broken her own word and allowed the Rum Preacher back into her husband's bed. Hector Bligh seemed so close to death himself. For this there were arguments to take up with God, but not right now. In a few minutes she would have a far more severe argument with someone else.

In the grocery shop people looked at her in a new way, with heads tilted and eyes that darted as her gaze met theirs. When a man went to live with a woman she became a sexual creature. *Widow Greenfield get man at last before the pokie dry up.* But this was not man but Devil. The Apostle spoke it in prophecy. The Widow was defiant. *Turn on a light in fi them house and every-*

body scramble like roach. Not even Lucinda could cast first stone. She knew her. Lucinda tried so hard to put up one face that she was probably hiding another. She had tried to steal the Widow's husband. The Widow remembered Lucinda eleven years ago, standing across the road from the wedding reception in her black veil and funeral dress, resembling a John Crow. Lucinda spied on the Greenfields when they were doing married people things. But the animosity ran deeper than that. Before marriage, before puberty.

At preparatory school, the girls called Lucinda plain, the boys called her ugly, but she imagined herself a beauty queen. Sessions in the outhouse were lessons in poise. It was her only relief from a recent whipping or escape from an upcoming one. She fixed a crown made of cardboard and tin foil to her head and grasped the scepter made from hibiscus bush as she crossed her legs at the ankle like the queen. On that day when Lucinda was on the throne, with her legs crossed and her ankles knotted up in her panty, she perfected her victory wave. The audience she imagined became real as the toilet door swung open. There in front and laughing so hard that tears ran down her face was the Widow Greenfield, then called Mary Palmer, along with Clarence, Buntin, soon to be Deacon Pinckney, Vixton Dixon, soon to be Brother Vixton, and Elsamire, soon to be deceased. Lucinda gripped her scepter trembling and crossed her legs tighter. Then she rose, regally, but the panty that had bound her legs together betrayed her and she tripped, falling face first in the muddy bush. Mary Palmer and her friends tumbled in the grass as well, grabbing their sides as if laughter threatened to burst from their bodies. They christened her Lucinda Queenie and off they went, with Mary's laughter a whirlwind barreling away. Lucinda did what she always did. She rose and straightened herself. Then she went inside, tore a page from her exercise book, and wrote a curse on every person who had wronged her, just as she saw her mother do. Her hatred was a fire that no man or God could put out. A fire that raged with their happiness and celebrated their tragedy. Lucinda Queenie made a deal with the Devil.

The Widow had not thought of the past in years, and found it odd that on this day she should remember.

"Hello? Hello? Excuse, please? Hello! Is you me talking to!"

"Me occupied with a customer, ma'am, so stop the cow ballin in me shop."

"Customer? But me no see no customer! Me is the only customer in here buying anything."

"Excuse me, ma'am."

"Yeah, you excuse you damn self and come back with half pound o sugar and two pound o flour."

"We don't have none."

"You don't have no flour or sugar?"

"We don't have neither. Go check somewhere else."

"You don't have neither, eeh? Then what you have in that bag by you foot mark flour, dog shit?"

"We don't have—"

"Listen here, don't take woman fi idiot! Is the flour bag that right at you foot and you telling me that you don't have none to sell," to which the shop-keeper, a rotund half-Chinese man in his forties, with thick glasses and thin-ning hair, came over to her. His face was less than a foot away from hers.

"No, you dry-up black bitch. We don't have none to sell to you."

The Widow pulled back. Eyes were upon her. She could feel every single one. A stare was a physical thing. Even after she grabbed her bag and left the shop, she could still feel their eyes on her, satellites for his eyes. They cut past skin and flesh and made bones tremble.

"Go with the Lord, ma'am."

At the mouth of the bridge they waited for her return. With every stomp of her feet—seven miles to the nearest shop and back—her anger grew, pump-ing with the swifter beat of her heart. But at the mouth of the bridge fury withered and fear returned. The Rude Boys were waiting. Now they were Rude Boys for Christ, but that made them no less rude. She passed them on the bridge in silence. The Widow clutched her bags close and continued with her head straight and eyes ahead. At a good distance she turned around and they were no longer on the bridge. The Widow willed the lump back down her throat when she realized that they were following. The leader, tall and fat, swung from one side of the road to the other. The Widow walked faster. The Rude Boys followed. They would kill her with little effort, but toy with her first; four cats with one mouse. A can tumbled ahead of her and banged against the sidewalk. Several stones, some hitting her shoe, followed. They kicked garbage, dried shit, and cans. She walked faster, almost tripping over one of the things that hit her foot. Their footsteps sounded like a march. The Widow ran, cursing her burden and the man who was the cause. Clutching the bags, she almost ran past the gate. By the time she struggled to free the latch, they were gone.

Lucifer was not about to leave Gibbeah without a fight. Even now his servants in darkness were congregating. Multiplying. Possessing. They were ready to celebrate the victory of the Prince of Darkness, *but no!* said the Apostle to a circle that had gathered around the twisted calf. The Five had dragged it to the side of the road only minutes before. "Satan, we're sending this abomination straight back to the Hell you brought it up from." The Five sprinkled the calf with kerosene and the Apostle set it ablaze. He prompted those who were on the choir to sing "How Great Thou Art." The Apostle spread his arms and prayed in tongues, but this was no Abba babba tongues. The fire, larger than expected, shot up through the dusk. The smell of kerosene and cow fat circled the village.

Lucinda followed him back to the church office, but the door was shut in her face. The keyhole was also shut. Leaving, she saw one of his red books left by the window.

"Apostle?"

The book's pages smelt of old dust. Lucinda suppressed a tiny cough. Inside was his handwriting: dashes, slants, curves, and strikes that sometimes fell off the page. Most she could not make out, but he wrote "secret flight" in bold, block letters.

EAS AND W ST SAME M GICK. SOLANUM S TH KEY. TO SECR T FL G T. I HAVE FOUND THIS T TH ALL O V R THE W LD. TO LEA E PLANE FOR ANOTH IT MUST BE B R E W ED. A BR W OR A TEA FROM TH SOLANU , OTH W SE KNOWN AS BLA CH D CALLALOO.

"Jesus Christ!"

The book slipped from her hands and fell. She bent down to pick it up but his hand got there first.

"Lucinda." He stared at her for several seconds, his brow knotted in a frown and his lips pressed so firm they disappeared in his beard. "You see anything in here written for you? Do you?" He held it up and looked at her. She looked away. "If you can't mind your own business . . ."

"Y-y-yes sah. Yes, Apostle."

"Good. And another thing."

"Apostle? Apostle?"

The Apostle winced, sucking air between clenched teeth as he shut his eyes tight. He grabbed his head with both hands and swayed left and right.

"Apostle?"

He spun away from her, staggering and swaying. York still clutched his head with both hands, groaning louder and louder. His legs buckled and his heels stomped hard on the floor. He reached out with his right hand as if to grab something unseen and staggered toward Lucinda's desk. York groaned, bellowed, and sucked air through gnashed teeth. He lurched into the desk and hit the edge with his knee.

"Goddamn to Hell!"

"Apostle?"

"Go."

"Apostle, you sickly?"

"GET OUT!"

She left without her handbag. He threw himself into the chair and buried his head on the desk. Had she stayed behind the closed door, Lucinda would have heard what sounded like sobbing.

Outside, the night burnt with cow flesh.

Sometimes Pastor Bligh bolted upright in the bed, cried out, and fell back into sleep. Other times it seemed as if he was beyond sleep, adrift, yet on the bed, with only ragged breathing to signify life. The Widow never slept for long. Hours were spent watching and mapping her fear to the rise and fall of his chest.

At two in the morning she stumbled out of the armchair beside his bed and the cold bowl of soup flew from her hands. Bligh had been yelling for minutes.

His eyes were wide open, seeing nothing. The room was blood. Something had gripped him. The Widow thought the Devil. The Rum Preacher pushed himself to the headboard with one hand, blocking his face with the other. He stopped screaming and collapsed. She hated him. Her spirit rose and fell with his and she hated him. Because of Bligh, the Widow's heart was undoing her. They had struck a deal, heart and mind, and now heart was cheating out. It had begun by tricking her into doing things like adding more sugar to the limeade and looking at old dresses in red, yellow, and blue. She wished she could punch a hole in her chest and yank the frigging thing out. The Widow had grown accustomed to death. The routine of death; the mossy, mothy grayness of it. God had taken away every man who had unfroze her heart.

She left him and went into the living room, making her way through the darkness. Through the window she saw the arched roof of Mr. Garvey's house move. Not until one of them flapped its wings and flew did she see that there was a multitude of them and they covered his roof, shed, fence, and gate.

John Crows.

Obeah was collective wisdom. The obeah man or woman was a dispenser of oils and spells, but also a collector of secrets. Ever since Clarence got the oil, Mrs. Johnson had to muffle her orgasmic screams with a pillow. Oil was responsible for the pregnancy of at least one of the Purdue sisters despite no known male inseminator. Poor little Elsamire, in a sudden fit of country madness, threw herself off a cliff in Port Antonio, and as her body slammed against the rocks, there was at least one once-jealous girl who knew that oil worked. Obeah was the suspected culprit, but nobody had ever seen it work that way. Nobody had ever seen it work in any way, *for them is all good God-fearing people. And who is you fi ask that deh question? What a piece o cheek!*

The Apostle made no mention of the calf or obeah. Rumors popped up at random, like bubbles in a brew. At the grocery, people whispered *Rolling Calf*. Unexplainable things were nothing new to Gibbeah. Only few remembered, and only faintly, that the Apostle's arrival had gone unexplained as well. All this excitement was too much for Lucinda, who translated it sexually and whipped herself before sleep. In the morning the cow's ashes were swept away by wind, leaving an almost perfect circle of burnt black.

The Rum Preacher leapt from his bed, his eyes white and infernal. He was screaming again. To the Widow, he seemed to say the same things over and over, but they were not words. They sounded like gargles or names hacked to pieces before they were spat out.

"Lucas! Lucas! Lucas!"

ROLLING CALF
Part Two

Go down Emmanuel Road
Gal an boy
Fi go broke rock-stone
Go down Emmanuel Road
Gal an boy
Fi go broke rock-stone
Broke them one by one
Gal an boy
Broke them two by two
Gal an boy
Finger mash don't cry
Gal an boy
Remember a play we deh play

The truck did late.
It did always late.
Late to come.
Late to leave.
Late to pick up the mash-up stone.
Late to go from where it come.
Usually is nuff of we that get the little day's work which go to helping out round the house.
Grandmother did do it, mother do it.

And pickney do it too.

Them lay out the big limestone rock pon the side of the road and we pick up we hammer and commence to broking.

Finga mash, don't cry. Remember a play we deh play.

We no know what them use the rock for.

Some say to make road. Some say to make rich white woman house. Nobody never ask cause country people take things as them be.

By the next morning the truck come and pick up what we broke up, but leave behind plenty, almost two hill of stone on the two side of Brillo Road near the bridge.

The truck did gone, but the Devil just come.

Yes sah! Word burst like fire pon dry grass say Mrs. Johnson making bun in the oven!

What you saying pon we earshole?

Yes baba! Rumor jump from her yard and race down the street and stop at Mrs. Fracas house, then Mrs. Smithfield house where it pick up two more story, then it hop and skip and jump from one yard to the next, then it race to the grocery shop where it bounce and bounce like American ball. And every time rumor bounce, the story pick up something new.

Well, everybody know say Mr. Johnson lose him nature ever since him come back from the war. Only thing him can do with it is piss.

True-true. Everybody know say that if she breeding, the baby better take after him mother hard or all Hell goin broke lose. If that baby ever look like the man who a dig her, then Clarence in some serious hataclaps. Then when even people who should know better start to say is really so, news bounce back say is not so. Is just sick she sick. Then news start bounce again, saying she kill the baby. Nuff woman, when them see say the blood stop run and them belly get sicky-sicky, start eat whole heap o green paw-paw to stop baby from borning.

That is nothing new, stillborn baby who mad say them never get born haunt plenty woman.

One time rumor say stillborn baby haunt Mrs. Smithfield so much that she have secret funeral round the back of her house and wash out her pokie with goat milk.

Then hi—everybody know say that when poor little Lillamae father mess with her and she start show that she eat green paw-paw. Mrs. Fracas say she see it, or she hear it.

Mrs. Fracas hear and see so much that she don't know if she see with her nose or hear with her eye. She say that is only when the box under Lillamae bed start stink up the whole house and dog start sleep outside her window that she sneak round the back of the house and bury the baby. A no nothing new.

But things was getting out of hand.

Tell we.

Mr. Johnson tell people that ever since the war when him used to sleep in the trench under gunfire and bomb and them things, no noise can wake him. Now Mr. Johnson is one big man. Bigger than Paul Robeson who sing Old Man River in that Showboat movie that play at the Majestic. Once him gone to sleep, him might as well be dead. But every night you hear whimpering coming from him room like when cat a cry.

Whimpering? Is more than that. Moaning and groaning. And grunting.

And the bedspring creaking fast, then slow, then fast again.

You know what it is and you ears feel wet.

For a man who sleep like him dead, Mr. Johnson up to whole heap of night activity in him bedroom.

Like is Mr. Johnson doin the activity.

But hi! Things that should a gone with night come catch people in the day. Heh-hay!

Now you know say Saturday is one bad day for Mr. Johnson.

Friday night worser.

People say is was a Friday night when him was marching in Normandy that everybody in him regiment get kill except him. Now every time Friday night start turn into Saturday morning him live it all over. Two months before, them see him burst through him house door and drop flat and roll, all the time screaming, "Blue company, out! Blue company, out!" When them finally find him, him already dig this big hole right behind somebody house and curl up in it covering him ears. Since then, him keep him World War to himself. Nobody too sure bout how certain things did happen, but here is the best guess.

Tell we.

Mr. Johnson head take him and him jump out of bed again to go join blue company when a explosion go off and him hit the ground. Him seeing trench instead of floor. Then him start crawl like lizard and go right under the marriage bed. That must be where him find things that never should a lost.

Holy Jesus our Heavenly Father!

Mrs. Smithfield hear the first noise. Mrs. Johnson scream something loud and Mr. Johnson scream back, "Then a who fah? After me no wear white brief." Then she say she don't know and him say that him goin kill her today, today, today.

Abba babba sicorsa tatta.

Then she start scream again and things start smash up. She bawling out like is the Devil over there killing her, and everywhere her screaming voice go, him Hellfire voice follow. "So one buddy no good enough, eh? Whoring nayga slut, I goin fix you bloodclaat business!" him say. She scream louder. People start gather outside the gate to watch God judgment. Lucinda race down to the church to call the Apostle. Mrs. Johnson begging somebody, anybody, to come save her because him goin kill her. More people outside the gate. Then we hear something else drop.

Drop?

Drop. Like when you drop meat. Then her door burst open and Mrs. Johnson jump out like she explode from cannon. But she stop when she see everybody outside her gate looking at her. Mrs. Johnson cover her breast with one hand and her pokie with the other. Her brassiere did tear open and her hair did pull up and wild, with some of her roller hanging off her head like Christmas tree. That was all she did wear. Her left eye did swell so big that it close up shut. She didn't know what to do. She look so fool that she couldn't even remember to feel shame. Then right in the middle of the quiet everybody hear something click. Mrs. Johnson know what it was right away and run off round the back. The second everybody see him, everybody scatter. Mr. Johnson bus through him door with him eye them black like sin. Him have on him war face. Nobody ever go near Mr. Johnson anytime him head take him, and them don't go for one reason.

When him come back from the war, them make him keep the rifle.

Him step through the gate and gone up the road.

Is Satan take over now.

Mr. Johnson don't say no word next. Him just bawl out like him is the wildest wild animal ever born. The rest of the people follow back o him, but way back cause nuff people was in the grocery when him was telling people bout friendly fire. But nobody did really have to follow, cause everybody know where him was going.

When the people see him coming them step out of the way. But the Apostle was coming. Apostle York come with Lucinda peeping from behind him frock like monkey. Mr. Johnson start huff and puff, but the Apostle block him way. Mr. Johnson shift left and the Apostle shift left. Mr. Johnson shift right and the Apostle shift right. Mr. Johnson shift left and grab him gun tighter. Him eye redder than red. Him was going kick down the Apostle to get to the man house.

"*Vengeance is Mine, saith the Lord,* Hugh. Give me the gun."

Mr. Johnson grab him gun tighter. Him finger lock pon the trigger and Mrs. Fracas scream and people start run. Him wasn't just goin kill Clarence, him was goin kill everybody who did know.

"Hugh, give me the gun."

We no understand why the Apostle so calm. Him talking to Mr. Johnson like him is some baby who pick up the wrong toy. Everybody who set to run now stop to watch. People fraid like puss, but them watch anyway. Except Mrs. Fracas. She run back to her house, with a trail of piss following her all the way to her door.

"Hugh, *vengeance is Mine,*" the Apostle say again. Everybody stare pon Mr. Johnson, who stare back pon the Apostle real hard.

"Hugh, does God have to show you who's God? Well, does He? Does He, Hugh?"

Mr. Johnson huffing and puffing for a long while. So long we feel like we living and dying between each huff and puff. Him turn round to look behind him and everybody jump. Him huff and puff two more time and stand still. Mr. Johnson stare down the Apostle and the Apostle stare down back. We waiting. Then him give the Apostle the gun. We hear a door slam from behind Clarence house. The Apostle wave him two finger and The Five come out of nowhere and run off behind the house. Clarence bawl out three time and the whole o we looking, except Mr. Johnson. Little time after that, them carry Clarence out to the front. Four of them grab one limb each and the last one hold him head up by grabbing him hair. Clarence did always red, but this morning him head did look like blood was goin burst out o him face. Them catch him wearing the same kind of white brief that start all o this. Them bring him to the Apostle. Mr. Johnson sit down at the side of the road like him studying the gravel. Clarence eye swirling round like him can't wake up.

"Clarence, I'm so disappointed in you," the Apostle say. "The Lord sees all, knows all. You're a fool and a sinner. The Lord have mercy on you.

"Beloved! Our brother, our, oh my Lord, what a shame it is to call this bastard our brother. A member of our church and still he chooses to reject the Lord and live a life of sin! Worse, he has corrupted another and made a mockery of holy matrimony. But listen to me, brethren. The man committed nothing illegal. He broke no laws. No, saints, he did something worse than that. He broke God's heart! If we punish a man who breaks man's law, what more should we do to a man who breaks God's heart? Can anybody tell me? What shall we do?"

Is supposed be 6:00. Some of we couldn't believe it, but even those who didn't believe come out to see. Some people frighten and some people think is joke. The rest of we saying that is God judgment and nobody else responsible but them two nasty naygas who defile the Temple of the Holy Spirit. Plus, an example must be made in Gibbeah that we are people of the Lord and disobedience will not be tolerated—is so the Apostle say. We did think that if anything would bring out Mr. Garvey and him nephews, this must be it. But him didn't come. The house stay shut up tight, with black curtain blocking all the window. Clarence laugh like this is the stupidest joke anybody ever tell him. Mrs. Johnson nah laugh though. The two of them under the cotton tree in the church cemetery. Brother Vixton use the cow rope to tie them up real good. Them look like them hanging from the branch even though them foot on the ground. Rope wrap round them wrist like how some rope use to wrap round people neck. Leave it to Vixton to have a whip save up from long time. Whip that him great-grandfather thief from white massa himself.

Clarence still a laugh?

Clarence take this thing make joke. Him still in him guilty brief and Mrs.

Johnson still in her guilty brassiere. Nobody no put no clothes on them. Some man never see pokie like Mrs. Johnson own, which never bush up.

She trim her bush for Clarence.

Some of the woman them a size up Clarence and one of them remember she always sell him size-thirteen boot. Mrs. Smithfield hear that and start look down pon him brief harder. Is 6:00 but the sun was never hotter. The little girl them laugh them little girl laugh. The boy them point. Everybody come out to see it, even those who didn't believe it.

What bout Pastor Bligh and the Widow woman?

Them never come.

Them goin get floggin next.

Mrs. Johnson start beg her husband so much that nuff people start to feel sorry for her. But then the Apostle remind we bout Bible Chapter Mark where the demons beg the Son of God, and if the Son of God did listen to all this begging, plenty people would be in Hell right now. That change we mind back.

She is the reason why the Devil take up residence in Gibbeah and we must cut it out! Cut it out! Cut it out! The Apostle also say that this is not just punishment but is also love, cause God punish who him love. That make we want the whipping worser. Then him point two finger at Brother Vixton.

Tell we what happen next although we know.

Vixton swing the whip and Mrs. Johnson scream like we never think she could scream. None of we ever get whipping yet, so none of we ever hear scream like that. Is not what we did think we was goin hear. Is not scream like when you dusting under the dresser and a rat jump out on you. Is not a scream like when you slam the door on you finger. Is not a scream like when you see thief in the backyard robbing you cabbage. Is something else. Like when Mrs. Fracas hear say the white people cows trample her little son and kill him.

By the third lash we see that this really a happen. Is ten lick she fi get and by lick number six the leather cut through her back and her black skin turn red. By number eight lash she stop scream, but she start drip. By number ten her knee them buckle and she out. She start to swing as if breeze pushing her. The rope around her wrist as white as where the skin start to strip off. Her eye them shut.

Clarence was to get twenty lash. All the time the Apostle giving God thanks, Clarence a cuss and cuss and bringing down Hellfire and damnation pon everybody in the village. The Apostle wave him two finger and Brother Vixton swing the whip like a hatchet chopping down a tree. Clarence chomp him teeth hard and shut him eye tight. Then him ask the Brother if that is the best that him can do.

That must did make Brother Vixton whip him worser.

True-true. Clarence start fight, but him couldn't do nothing but bruise him wrist under the rope. The white rope turning red. Mrs. Johnson eye still shut. Clarence not saying nothing, but him grind him teeth every time the leather lash him. By lash eight, him skin all cut up and him back look like when you slice up a pig. Vixton give him a extra hard lash and the front of Clarence brief explode with piss that run down him leg.

By lash thirteen, him gone from a white brief to a red brief. The people silent. Even the little pickney. Them either looking away or looking right past the cotton tree as if nobody swinging from it. Brother Jakes grab him boy and force him to look. Brother Vixton stop whipping and everybody just shudder with relief, but then him look pon the Apostle and the Apostle raise two finger. By lash fifteen, Clarence leg them start buckle too. Him head drop down and both him and Mrs. Johnson start swing. Mr. Johnson turn away, but the Apostle grab him and turn him round back. By lash twenty, the whip split. The Apostle say that God already will Vixton to make another bullwhip.

God judgment done. Some of we start scratch we back and everybody feel a way. The Apostle say this is a great day for Gibbeah cause we stand up for the Son of God who name we not to say. And we do a brave thing by saying no to sin. We see Mrs. Johnson blood and Clarence blood and the two of them blood mix together and blood up the cotton tree, the ground, and the whole cemetery. This is the first time it feel like not even a dead man place have any peace. The Apostle say to leave them til 10:00 in the night and then take them down and clean them up. Mrs. Smithfield shudder when him tell she fi clean them up.

God judgment a no play-play judgment.

God not romping with we.

We go home, leaving them pon the tree. None of we have nothing to say, so we just go into we own house and shut the door. Mr. Johnson go home and people who live near him say him cry all night.

The next morning them find another calf.

ROLLING CALF
Part Three

The Rum Preacher woke up ravenous. The Widow readied herself like an eager virgin. The table was laid before him and he ate with fury. They said nothing. He gorged himself on mackerel stewed in coconut milk, johnnycakes, roasted breadfruit, steamed cabbage, strips of bacon, potato pudding, and coffee, which she had roasted herself. The Widow had placed her chair in the room's darkest spot. From there she looked on as the Rum Preacher came back to life. His hunger consumed the table, leaving upturned dishes and spilled gravy in his wake. And he wanted more.

Deacon Pinckney's son found the calf. Hopping and skipping like a masterless gig, the child tripped over its hoof. Not afraid, he prodded it. The calf refused to come back to life, which left the boy with no choice but to revive it with his magic wand, just as Mandrake did in the comic strip. But the wand was no help either. The boy thought the calf strange, lying dead in the cornfield with the head upside-down. Lucinda saw it next and immediately threw herself to the ground in a fit of intercession for the soul of Gibbeah. Preceded silently by The Five, Apostle York came to see.

"Anybody knows whose cow this is? Whose brand is that? On the backside, whose brand?"

"Massa Fergie, Apostle. Him keep them for the MacMillans in Brownstown."

"The MacMillans?"

"The MacMillans, sah. A white family who live down a Brownstown. Them rich plenty."

"Rich?"

"Like Solomon, Apostle."

"And white, you say?"

"Like Santa Claus belly."

"So is white people, mammon-lovers, bringing the Devil to Gibbeah?"

"Me no know if them like fish, sah."

"What? No, not salmon, mammon."

"If you say so a so, Apostle."

"Find me this . . . this Massa Fergie. He comes to church?"

"Him used to, sah, but when lightning strike the . . . when, ah . . . it . . . ah . . . kill the other man, him take over the blacksmith shop and leave the cows to do what them do."

"I see. Anyway, bring this man to me."

By now a crowd had gathered around them, breaking corn plants with their feet. A few confirmed that this was indeed obeah let loose. Others were just relieved that there was something, some new distress, to take their minds off the smell of whipped flesh. Wickedness was begetting wickedness. The Five pulled the old man from the crowd and presented him to the Apostle.

"Good morning, my brother. Is this your cow?"

The man said no, figuring without fully knowing that whatever yes could mean, it certainly wasn't good. He repeated no; after all, there was no way any cow of his could have been born with an upside-down head and he not notice. The Apostle kicked the cow's head and Gibbeah shook. He pointed at the brand on the cow's backside.

"I'm no Balaam, but this ass says different."

The old man stooped down to look. Nerves came down on him in a flush. He knew he was being watched. He spat on the ground. "Me say is not my cow."

"It's your brand. That is your mark. This is your beast. Do you deny that that is your mark, Master Fergie?"

"Is my—I mean, is the MacMillan brand, but is not my cow."

The Apostle stared at him, his eyes wide open like a child. Massa Fergie spat again and watched it roll in dirt. The show of defiance wasn't enough; the Apostle was still looking at him. Silence hovered, feebly interrupted by gulps, shuffles, and fidgets.

"You're right, old man. This is not your cow. This cow have a new mark, written by Satan himself! All you people who love your signs and your wonders, wonder about this. Who inverts God's promise? Who take everything God meant for good and turns it to bad? Who twists good into evil just as easily as he twisted this cow's neck? Well, who? Is there no voice in Gibbeah?"

One by one, a chorus of "Satan" and "the Devil" popped off all over the cornfield.

"A spirit of witchcraft is on this village, you hear me, but mark my words, we're going to cut it out! Cut it out! Cut it out!"

Lucinda's back began to itch.

"Burn it."

Followed in single file by The Five, the Apostle went back to the church.

The Rum Preacher ate his way to Sunday. It excited the Widow just to keep up. Bligh was making himself young and her too. Nowadays she decided not to curse such things. When he prayed, which he did often, she prayed as well, not to God or to him, but to the space between them. She mixed the beverage sweeter, holding back the Seville orange and pouring extra spoonfuls of sugar. She rolled the dumpling dough softer. Her touch became light, freed from expressing bitterness in every gesture. Her hair showered down on her shoulders. She was wearing blue. The Pastor was blind to his own handiwork.

"You goin out in that hot sun today?"

"No."

"Oh."

That was all they said for the rest of the day. In the past, silence would be thickened with tension, but now it took on the grace of familiarity. The Pastor and the Widow had developed a way of un-speak that seemed better than words.

A man wore forgiveness in a way unlike shame, even though both possessed a similar lowness. But in that lowness was no despondency or self-hate, only submission and release. Bligh was beyond pride and self. The Lord had killed him. He was reborn for the second time, for one purpose. He would take nothing for the journey but the knowledge that he would never be left nor forsaken. Fear of the Lord was the beginning of wisdom, but humility before the Lord was evidence of it. The Rum Preacher would be ready. But not today.

Lucinda rushed back to her house, hushing herself and wrapping the bandages tighter. The iodine had not stopped burning. The night before, a million screams imploded in her mouth. She had shut her lips tight, lest they escaped while the whip sliced across her back. Someone was making her young too. In the past, she could explain it as a consequence of her unclean days. But now there was an everlasting heat that she could not whip out. So she whipped harder. Lucinda was a simple woman who concluded simply. But here was something that seemed monstrous. Something so beyond herself. More than once she had come close to letting her fingers have their way again; all ten digits finding points of pleasure in the fleshy folds of her dark vagina. She could smell in herself the rawness of fish. It disgusted her, yet brought fuel to her heat. She was a simple woman who concluded simply. If one spoonful did not cure, then two would do. If ten lashes could not cure, the solution was twenty. She whipped harder. By her stripes she would be healed. Lucinda stuffed her mouth with sponge and showered her back with iodine to let the wounds scream. God was not pleased, but he would be. Of her sacrifice, she was sure of it. Lucinda was to be the bride of Christ but her ring finger got lost in a thatch of pubic hair. It was that damn Apostle. Him and those bold red books and the bold red tip of his circumcision.

When she awoke the next day, her fever had left its damage. The bed was soaked with sweat, iodine, and blood. She wrapped herself in more bandages, so many more that the normally poised woman now seemed to develop a hunchback.

The Apostle cracked his knuckles on the podium and addressed the congregation directly. He declared that there were demons in the church and threw himself into a fit of tongues. He declared that there was a spirit of witchcraft in the village that had to be broken for the children's sake. He commanded the spirits gone in the name of the Father. Cows were God's creatures, as bright and beautiful as everything else He made. The Apostle reclaimed the cow in the name of the Father. The congregation whooped and hollered. Then he called to the altar all those with a burden on their hearts.

A few came up and the Apostle laid hands. He commanded one woman to let go of bitterness and slaughter the spirit of hate that had been killing her from the inside. He commanded her to take her virginity back in the name of the Father. She lifted her dress and the Apostle touched it, shouting to the congregation that he felt her hymen grow back. She writhed, shook, and screamed as soon as his hand touched her forehead. Then she fell to the floor, almost missing the hands of one of The Five who was there to catch her fall. She screamed again, more than her throat could bear, and began to cough.

"I command you to come out of her in the name of the Father!" he shouted. "Spirit of witchcraft, I command you to come out of her in the name of the Father! Spirit of whoredom begone!" The woman bucked and bellowed as if her belly had begun to split open. Foam came to her mouth. Her eyes were lost inside her skull. At the same time another woman began running from one end of the altar to the other and back, screaming, "Come out o me! Come out o me!"

The Apostle pointed two fingers and The Five went after her. He laid hands and she too fell bawling and screaming. The church was in uproar, but the organist kept playing and the choir kept singing. The ladies of the front row leapt to their feet and interceded in tongues. Others followed, rising with their arms spread wide and eyes shut tight. And yet there were others, disturbed and frightened, who did nothing but watch. By the end of the service, eight, all women, were delivered from evil spirits.

The noise was such that even Pastor Bligh listened from his window. He threw himself into a fit of praying too, but for a different purpose.

The Apostle declared that the curse upon the cows had been lifted, and from now on there would be no obeah cows. No more guzum. But, he added, these things were only the fruits and branches; the whole root had to be dug up. The obeah man. The Devil man. The fornicator with the whore of Babylon. The Antichrist—oh yes! Men could be witches too! Look at poor Clarence, who was so caught up in the Devil's schemes that he corrupted a married woman in the process. Since the Devil and his children did their nefarious deeds at night, at night they would wait, and at night they would cut it out!

Some feared and some hoped that just this once, night would renege on its promise to come. But come night did, draping her dew-wet, cricket-chirping canopy over Gibbeah. The torches were lit and the people were ready. Tonight they would go into the Devil's camp and take back what he stole. By the blood of the Father.

Massa Fergie feared for his cows. He was late. Night caught up with the herd on the road and he beat them hard, terrified that he might meet the Devil there. Or Rolling Calf. Maybe somebody should have told the cows that they had reason to fear. They trotted along with easy procession despite the whip, doing as they always did when it got too dark to see grass. By the time they arrived at the bullpen, all had come home save one. He ran back into the darkness after the cow.

It took the Apostle's holy thunder and a couple verses from the Book of Daniel to mix the crowd's fear and rage into a mob. They moved as one beast. From above they looked like a dragon who spat fire. Tonight, tonight was when the Devil would be defeated. The Apostle began the procession, raising praising songs along the way. Midway he fell back and let the crowd, now on their own mad momentum, pass him. The Rum Preacher watched as they marched past his window.

The cow had trapped her horn in a fence that separated pasture from river. Massa Fergie pried the horn loose, but the cow refused to move. The man cussed and pushed. He bracketed the cow's backside with his hands and pushed with his feet. The cow moved, but only slightly. Massa Fergie pushed again, but dew had made the cow's hide slippery. He slipped and grabbed the cow's tail to break his fall.

"See him deh!"

"Me did tell you say it was him."

I went back into the enemy's camp

"Watch the man a do nastiness with the cow!"

And took back what he stole from me

"Obeah!"

"Nasty man! Watch how him was feeling up the cow! You see him? You see him?"

"Nastiness!"

I said I took back what he stole from me

"Lawd, him a work guzum pon the cow!"

He's under my feet, he's under my feet

Massa Fergie fled but was run down. A circle of flames surrounded him with hisses, shouts, and curses. The fires created shadows and he could see no faces. These were the demons from Hell that had come for the cow. *He's under my feet, he's under my feet.* From the fire and black came a stick that struck him in the face. He fell, horrified, as the mass of fire and darkness jumped him. *He's under my feet, he's under my feet.* The mass hollered and screamed and stomped and shouted and spat. *He's under my feet, he's under my feet.* He did not feel his left leg break nor his ribs crack one after the other, nor his nose crush, nor his temple echoing the force of several blows; the strike to the back of his head drowned the others out. *He's under my feet, he's under my feet.* The crowd hit, stomped, and burnt. *He's under my feet, he's under my feet.* Massa Fergie screamed twice, then no more. But when one of the mob released his hand and it fell to the ground, the thud had the shock of thunder. They pulled back. The mob broke apart into individuals separated by what they had done. While rage could be communal, guilt was always personal. The people ran away with their torches. From above it looked like a clump of fire had exploded into tiny, scattering embers. The Apostle stepped over the body and went his way. Massa Fergie lay in the dirt, his skull crushed and ribs bashed in as if trampled by a bull.

UP! JUMPED THE DEVIL

hank you, Choir. Church, you may be seated."

"Ahh. Uhum."

"Hmph."

"My God."

"My good God."

"Church, I used to think I was a man of many words, but you people, you've . . . you've . . . I'm at a loss. It's a good thing that the Lord our God is an understanding God. A merciful God. It's a good thing that He looks beyond that face and sees all hearts, because if God were like me He would think that the Devil took charge of praise and worship. This couldn't be a full gospel church. I see more praise going on at a funeral! At a Catholic church!

"But God. It's a good thing the Lord knows your burden. Church, I too know your burden because I am God's voice. Your heart is heavy; the lowest of the low, I know, my heart is heavy too. I was there on Thursday too, you know. I was there when the Lord spoke His justice.

"We're afraid.

"We're upset.

"We're distraught. Even more of us are confused and just about everybody is ashamed. Be truthful before the Lord, you, we are all ashamed. I know what you're thinking. Thou shalt not kill, I know. That night is playing over and over in your head like that Devil music they keep sending over from foreign. But, beloved, I'm only going to say this once.

"WAKE UP! What do you think this is? Pin the tail on the donkey, church? This is war!

"High time some of you in here get off your blessed assurance. God didn't come here to heal the sick, He came with a sword! We're tearing down the kingdom of Satan! We launching D-Day on the shores of Hell. We're going into the enemy's and taking back what he stole. Oh Abba babba a maka desh—I wish I had a God-fearing church. The Devil is not your boyfriend. Satan is not some naked red boy with a tail and a pitchfork! The Bible says he comes to steal, kill, and destroy! Is either him or us! So what's it going to be, Gibbeah, him or us? The Devil or the saved? But the Lord says, thou shalt not kill.

"Well, church, what if I tell you that was no man that you killed? You believe me when I talk to you, Lucinda? Listen to me. God made man in His own image, but He made the Devil in His own image too. And His demons. You babes in Christ, don't you see what's happening? I know what the problem is, your hearts are too hard! If your hearts weren't so hard, God wouldn't have to put so much pressure on you. Don't you see? Church?

"God is opening your eyes, so that you see sin the way He sees it. What does Leviticus Twenty, verse fifteen say? I read, *And if a man lies with a beast he shall SURELY be put to death.* And after cows, my brother and sisters, what's next, boys? Is that where you want that pervert's penis to end up?

"Turn with me to Exodus, Chapter Thirty-two, and verses twenty-six to twenty-nine:

Then Moses stood in the gate of the camp, and said, Who is on the Lord's side, let him come unto me. And all the sons of Levi gathered themselves together unto him.

And he saith unto them, Thus saith the Lord God of Israel, Put every man his sword by his side, and go in and out from gate to gate throughout the camp, and slay every man and his brother, and every man his companion, and every man and his neighbor.

And the children of Levi did according to the word of Moses, and there fell of the people that day about three thousand men.

"Follow me. What did Moses do to the Israelites who were worshipping the Golden Calf? He butchered every single one. Three thousand. And yet look at us, crying over one. God is God. And He will kill your own mother if she is serving the kingdom of darkness. Had the Israelites refused to obey the Lord, do you think they would have made it to the promised land? And if you don't kill the sin that so easily entangles, how will you ever come into the true promise of God?

"Christianity is not a romping business. Men of God, this is war! And the Devil don't fight fair. Look at what that Massa Fergie was doing. Cut it out! Cut it out! Cut it out! If people come here with the smell of Satan, send them right back out. Anything that is of the Devil needs to be driven right back to Hell.

"And the quickest way to send something back to Hell is to kill it."

The Apostle saw him first. The second he passed Mrs. Fracas, the Rum Preacher sparked a disquiet in her that took over the church. The congregation was silent, but standing. Bligh was in his white suit, all clean and sparkling except for the right shoulder that bore the weight of a filthy burlap sack. The Five came from five directions on the Apostle's orders, but to the shock of all, Bligh raised his hand high and pointed two fingers. All five stopped. Bligh marched slowly to the altar and stopped directly in front of Apostle York.

"You're like a boil on my arse, Bligh. I squeeze you out, you grow back. I drive you away, you keep coming back. Maybe I should just whip you? You think I should? Maybe I should—"

"Then I'd be lucky, cause word is you whipping young men and killing old ones. But who you going to kill for this?"

He threw the weight down but held onto the sack. It fell to the floor. Those who were closest screamed first. Brother Vixton vomited from the smell. The congregation, most of whom had not seen what he threw down, stormed out of the church anyway, knocking down chairs, benches, the christening fountain, and the children. Within seconds, the church was empty, save for the Rum Preacher, Apostle York, and the goat, cold and muddy with a head twisted upside down, yet seamless with the body. Mud marked the floor. The stench of death woke the altar. The Apostle looked up, furious. The Rum Preacher could see right through his eyes to a second face. Before words were said, a wind whipped itself up into a tempest and slammed the doors shut.

PART TWO

LUCINDA

A week shy of her tenth birthday, Lucinda's papa struck her mother, called her a whore, and disappeared like Nicodemus, a thief in the night. Lucinda kept herself awake for several nights after that, waiting for his return. Her mother said he had left because his daughter was ugly and impudent. That was her earliest memory.

Little girl Lucinda was at school, fidgeting with her uniform as she sat at her desk. An hour had passed since the bell rang and the school was empty. She heard the breeze whistling through the louver windows. On the floor below the blackboard was a stick of orange chalk. Usually, she would have leapt for the thing, shoved it down her pocket, and ran straight home where she would teach the plants how to write, in between beating off every single leaf with her belt. Otherwise the silence would have scared her out. She had never been the last to leave the classroom before. The room had never looked so huge. With children in them, desks seemed to be alive. But here, with the wind whistling and the noon brilliance fading, they were coffins with legs. She had been holding her piss for an hour. A cramp would come back, sometimes mild, sometimes monstrous, and she'd squeezed her thighs tight, hoping to send the piss back up. But little drops escaped and damped her bloomers.

They had laughed at her. Even Elsamire, who shared her desk, covered her mouth to hide the slowly growing front tooth. Now their laughs seemed to come back every time the piss came back. She squeezed her thighs tighter, clenched her teeth, shut her eyes, and counted backwards from one hundred to one. If only she could get to one, then the piss would go back. If she could just get from 100 to 99, 98, 97, 96, 95, 94, 93, 92, 91, 90, 89

88, 87, 86, 85, 84, 83, 82, 81, 80

79, 78, 7—

"Lucinda! What in Heaven's name you doing in here chile? What kind of idle skylarking you up to?"

The teacher was upon her before Lucinda could speak. She was so tall that she seemed to scrape the ceiling with her hair. She had no eyes. The thick glasses reflected light in Lucinda's face. But her hands were strong. When she gave you a beating, you stayed beat. The teacher clutched Lucinda's cheeks and squeezed.

"You ill?"

Lucinda shook her head.

"Toothache? All them godforsaken sweeties rotting your mouth?"

Lucinda shook her head.

"What about your house? You mother lose her head again?"

Lucinda shook her head.

"Then what is the reason for this dillydallying? Look how long school dismiss?"

There were five voices with which an adult spoke. Lucinda recognized them, because her mother had only one. Mary Palmer's mother had three. There was the "dinner ready" voice, the "get off the veranda that a just clean" voice and the "never mind, baby, it soon get better" voice. No matter what was said, everything that came from the teacher's mouth sounded like an inquisition. The "you're idle and you're evil" voice.

"Girl chile, do it look like is breeze me talking to? Speak up, little girl, why you not going home?"

Lucinda would not speak.

"I losing my patience with you. Why pickney ears must always hard? Why unu always begging for a beating?"

Lucinda looked down in her lap.

"You want problem? Is problem you round here looking for? Answer when big people speak to you! I will give you nuff problem. Get up this blinking instant. Me say, git up!"

The teacher grabbed Lucinda by the collar and yanked her up. She screamed as the bench rose with her for a second then fell back, tearing off her uniform at the waist. Now you have you throne, Lucinda Queenie,

Elsamire had said, chuckling as she waved the bottle of glue at Mary and the others. Lucinda was confused until she tried, one hour later, to go to the bathroom.

"Oh for Heaven's sake, what is wrong with these pickneys! Is the Devil in them, Jesus, must be the Devil. Them know how much money me pay for that glue? Them think say glue cheap? Straight a Kingston me, meself go buy the glue and look how them waste it. Idle hands, Jesus. Devil's workshop for sure. Devil's workshop. Gal, go to you bloodclaat yard before me give you reason to stay. And if you tell anybody what me just say, is me and you tomorrow."

Outside the wind whispered laughter as Lucinda's legs felt the warm stream of piss.

She went home on secret roads. She crossed the river instead of the bridge and waited until evening. Her mother's house was not part of the Gibbeah Plan. It hung like the other shacks on the outskirt but still within the boundary of the river. There were two rooms, a bedroom for her mother and the kitchen-dining-sitting room that was the bedroom for Lucinda. The house was overrun with old furniture stolen from an abandoned plantation. Luxurious red chairs blackened by coal and black magic. Four of these chairs were scattered around the room as if they had placed themselves. A bamboo coffee table with a vase of plastic flowers sat in the center of the room. There was a gray Formica dining table to the right but no chairs, and the tabletop was littered with dried plants, glass jars filled with vinegar and water, spoiled mangos, and shriveled apples. Lucinda opened one of the cupboards and pushed past the jar filled with lizard skins and dog paws to find the last bag of police-button cookies.

Now to figure out how to slip outside without stirring her mother, whose room she had to pass. Her mother sounded busy. Maybe she would not see. Lucinda tiptoed past the room but looked when she heard the comb fall and bounce on his shoe. She followed his legs, moving up from one dot of curled body hair to the next. She moved up to his sweaty buttocks that clenched tight when he plunged in and spread wide when he pulled out. She moved up to his shirt, so orange that the glow tinted her mother's feet, both of which where on the man's shoulders. Her mother was on the dresser, her sweaty back greasing the mirror as the man rammed inside her. Lucinda imagined his cock as stubby as he was plunging in and out of her mother's vagina that was as loose as she was. Then he shifted and she saw it for a second, his penis disappearing into her mother and his jerky balls bouncing like elastic. Her mother had two gentlemen a week, sometimes three. By the time Lucinda looked in the dresser mirror, he had long seen her. The man raised one of his bushy eyebrows and smiled, rounding his fat face. He gyrated, swirling his hips and thrusting harder, as her mother held on.

"Woi! Woi, you donkey sweet, Daddy. Woi, me womb a shif. Take it easy with you donkey-la-la. Easy with you donkey-la-la."

The man grunted and stepped away.

"Come, black bull, give me the milk."

The man grunted again. Lucinda heard little drops fall to the floor.

"God no like when man spill him seed, bitch."

"God no like when you fuck for free either, donkey la-la."

"If me hafi pay money," he said, throwing the bills at her crotch, "then the pussy better more tight. How bout fi her own next time?"

"Fi who? What you talking bout?"

The man motioned to the mirror but the woman turned to the doorway, to the blur of Lucinda running away.

"What the—"

Lucinda sat outside on the steps eating police-button cookies. The force came so sudden that she felt nothing. The bag of cookies flew high in the air and landed in the dirt after she did, hands first, then face, as she skidded in the dust. Her mother nearly lost balance after kicking her.

"Nasty nayga bitch."

Lucinda knew the underbelly of the country. She knew the secret springs, winding roads, and invisible spirits more than anyone twice her age. Most she had learned from her mother. Two weeks later, on a moon-tinted night, Lucinda helped her mother brew the callaloo tea, then watched her drink. They were behind the house, close to the river to hear the flow, but hidden between trees so thick that no light could be seen. Her mother grabbed a bottle filled with river water, took some into her mouth, and spat into the bonfire. As the vapor vanished, so did she.

* * *

Lucinda had stopped speaking to her classmates after the pit toilet incident, but spoke the day before Christmas Eve. There was nothing remarkable to the day. Some passed it with lethargy, some with industry. But Elsamire, who sat beside her in class, was dead.

They found her on the rocks, by the spit of the sea. She had landed with violence, her body exploding like a smashed tomato. Above, back on the cliff, looking down, were her fellow students of the school outing, including Lucinda, who whispered to Mary, "Ah bet she wish she could a fly."

She had seen the body, but it was at Elsamire's funeral, where the casket was closed, that Lucinda saw the devastation of death. She vomited on one of Mr. Garvey's nephews, infuriating those around her for trying to steal attention at the poor little girl's funeral. They wouldn't have known, but her mother knew. She raised her chin and looked down at her daughter from the ridge of her nose.

Lucinda went home to her cot and fell asleep. When she awoke, night had fallen and a candle burnt in the room, throwing jagged shapes on the wall. One of the shapes broke away from the others and sat down beside her.

"Me know what you did," her mother whispered. Lucinda said nothing. "You hearin me? I say, I know what you did."

"Mummy?"

"Don't Mummy me. You think you fool everybody? You nearly fool me too until me see say me missing a few ingredients. Special ingredients. Things you mix and brew if you want a certain bitch out of the picture."

"Out of the picture, Mummy?"

"Go on, play fool to catch wise, but I know you. It start sweet you, don't it? Me see it in you face. You starting to like how blood taste. Make sure what happen a night no come back in day."

Lucinda sat alone at her desk for the rest of the year, never approached by anyone.

Adolescence was brutal for all except Clarence. His looks were miraculous, especially considering the ugliness of both parents. Pretty and ugly were loose words in Gibbeah, and as such, his beauty had as much to do with light skin and pink lips as anything else. Pity about the picky negro hair, his mother would say. His growth was a matter of pride, and shame for others. Clarence knew this from the day the boys stopped bathing together. They had stripped naked as they always did and dove into the frigid water screaming and laughing. But as Clarence climbed out, the other boys knew for the first time that he was different. They saw a patch of hair where there wasn't before, hair that they didn't have, and it was red. Lucinda saw the red hair too. A day would not pass where she did not sneak down to the river and hide under the cover of banana leaves as she watched the boys frolicking naked in the water. She watched as day by day all the boys stopped coming to the river except Clarence.

"Them things you want to do, you can do to me," she said to him from the river bank, half hiding in the shadow of banana trees. Clarence knew where to look. He had been watching her watching him for months.

"Oh? You think so? You don't even have titty yet," he said. He waded through the water toward her. Lucinda tried not to look at his red patch.

"Is not titty you goin use, or you didn't know?"

"What? Look yah, cross-eye chi-chi, me know everything."

"Then show me, nuh?"

"You want me to show you big-boy things? You think you ready for big-boy things? Alright, big girl, see me here."

"No now. Tonight."

"Little girl catch her fraid."

"Me not fraid! Is you fraid. Me say tonight."

"Tonight, then."

"Me want it in the cemetery."

"The cemetery?"

"The cemetery. Or you nah get the pokie."

It turned out that Clarence knew nothing of female genitals. He cursed her tightness for minutes until he remembered that he too had an anus. When he finally stuck her aright, he pushed her down on a dirty concrete grave. His hips slammed into hers a few times before he pulled out and sprayed her thighs with semen. Then he left her in the cemetery. She heard her papa's footsteps. Lucinda cried for days.

A week before Lucinda's twenty-second birthday, her mother found Jesus. She told Lucinda to throw away all the witchery things, and she did, keeping only some of the jars and potions for herself. She spent the next two years beside her mother, wearing white as she wore, standing when she stood, shaking when she shook, and screaming *Hallelujah!* when she screamed. Her mother had a second stroke, but was still coming to church—praise God. *Now if only Lucinda would go get herself a man before her pokie dry up and she can't have no pickney. Look how she make good man like Mr. Greenfield get way and go married that Mary girl who live in her dead mother house.*

"Lucinda, go cream you hair."

"Lucinda, God don't need no wife."

"Lucinda, you think is only pissing it make for?"

"Lucinda, what you doin round the back? If me catch you with no spirit business, I goin broke up you backside in this house."

"Damn fool you is, fi make man like Mr. Greenfield get way. And a town man at that. You know say him buy Mary Palmer house from Mr. Garvey and give she?

"Lucinda?"

"Me reading me Bible, Mummy."

As a Kingston man who had experienced piped water, Mr. Greenfield resented bathing by the river. But he and Mary Palmer were not married and she would not have a man getting naked in her mother's house. At least he was alone. As he washed himself, what should he hear but the indelicate splashing of Lucinda, who had come to wash herself too? Her polka dot dress around her neck, hanging like a noose.

"Me know you want to do nastiness with me," she said.

She was a church-going sister who was known as such. Nobody who knew Day Lucinda could find out about Night Lucinda. But as she released her buttocks to his coarse hand, a feeling came over her that in the past had only come from spirits. Lucinda reached to embrace, but he kept her away and they stood apart at the head, apart at the feet, slamming in the middle. When he came, he stepped away and spilled his seed into the river. She went over to him, rubbing her breasts on his shoulder. "So me and you goin married now?"

Greenfield looked at her eyebrows, raised for pity above her crossed left eye. He burst into a laugh that bounced all over the gorge through which the river ran. He pushed her away and she lost balance. When she fell backways in the river he walked off, not bothering to dress himself beyond a towel. She could hear him laugh all the way up to Mary's house.

Not long after that, on the day Lucinda helped her wash, her mother collapsed in the river. Bowing under a pregnant noon sun, the left side of her body went dead and she stumbled into rough water. Her mouth was half speaking, her eyes half blind, and her body half asleep. Lucinda watched as river currents ran over her mother and she drowned. Despite having use of only half her body, the woman might have saved herself were it not for Lucinda, whose pinning foot never left her mother's head until water forced its way into her lungs and killed her in jerks. There was to be no funeral. The night welcomed Lucinda back. In a bonfire she threw lizard skins, cat skeletons, and a dog's paw that her mother had saved in vinegar. Mary and Mr. Greenfield were married the next day.

Lucinda, having resigned herself to never again experience the misery of a man, took over Sunday school. Mary Greenfield would never have children and her marriage died long before her husband did, killed by stillbirths, mistrust, and jealousy.

Both women now found themselves compelled by men they barely understood. The wind nudged the Widow from her sleep and blew toward the church. Outside, noon burnt in silence. She knew that something had happened. The Widow ran to the church.

THE RECOVERY

The Widow Greenfield and Lucinda met in the church as they came to take their men away. Both men were unconscious and the building was at peace. The Rum Preacher lay in the aisle with benches scattered all around him. His white suit was covered in dirt and filth and his body had the heaviness of death. The christening pool at the rear of the church had been toppled over and water covered the floor. She grabbed him by the shoulders and pulled.

Lucinda screamed. She could not find the Apostle. There was a tower of rubble at the altar from the broken podium, wood planks that had been forced free, tapestries that had been torn down, and pieces of the organ. At the bottom was a stiff hand that pointed two fingers. She leapt over chairs and benches and pulled away with the strength that came with panic. The Apostle had a gash above his forehead and a line of blood that divided his face. Lucinda turned and glared at the Widow, but she was almost out the door. The Widow pulled the Rum Preacher through the door as the wind waited. Outside, John Crows had gathered on the steeple and the cross. The road was empty.

That night the Widow was prepared for the town's vengeance. She refused to light the candle, preferring the protection of darkness. Night swept down with stealth, unconcerned with the events of the day.

She had laid him in the room her husband was supposed to have died in. She imagined that she could smell Bligh's presence in the room now. That depressed her even more. She never smelt her husband's presence until he died. This would be what God would give her, grief. She cursed God under her breath, and the Rum Preacher, who made her wear blue.

Bligh's sleep was not like sleep. Nor was it like death. Nor was it like before, when he would jump up and scream from nightmares and fall back into the bed. This was different. His hands were cold, but his heart, when she touched his chest, beat swiftly as hers did when she was frightened. She pulled up a chair beside his bed and sat there until sadness lulled her to sleep.

The scratching jolted her awake. A branch swung against the window, scraping the glass. She rose and went to the window to see a John Crow flying away into the night. The Pastor was in the position she last saw him before she fell asleep. His hands to his side, his body stiff, but something was different. His eyes were wide open.

"Hector, Jesus Christ! Hect—"

She ran over to him and grabbed his hand. He said nothing, staring at the ceiling.

"Hector?"

She waved her hand over his face. He was not awake. The Widow wished right there that she still had a hardened heart.

Lucinda had put the Apostle to bed. That was no easy task, the Apostle was the heaviest man she had ever held, heavier than all the drunken men she had helped her mother throw out of the house. He was not dead and that filled her with hope, but he did not respond to her begs or cries, not even those made to the Lord Himself. Lucinda had long resolved to never again experience the misery of a man, but misery overcame her, like a plague or a great spirit. Day Lucinda took off his jacket and shoes, and as she looked at his pants, Night Lucinda entered her heart.

Lying flat on his back, his crotch seemed to have risen like a new mountain. A black hill between the huge ridges of his thighs. She forced herself to return to grief, but failed. She thought of her back and of the whipping, but neither could take her mind away from his bulge, hidden in black pants. She prayed for herself and left the room.

Outside in the dark, the half moon saw her. In the silver light, Lucinda saw herself for what she really was. A beast, not the false creature in church clothes. The moon knew that she spoke to Sasa and rubbed goat's blood on her breast. Far below grief was lust, and like any other sin, it came with opportunity.

Inside, the Apostle had not moved. Lucinda watched the rise and fall of his chest and the rise of other things that did not fall. She took deep breaths and closed her eyes. *God will punish you for your wickedness,* said Day Lucinda. *Touch where life come from,* said Night Lucinda. She sat down on the side of the Apostle's bed and touched his feet.

Just this once, the Widow wished she knew the things of the spirit. Perhaps then an angel would come and tell her what had happened. She was a woman of reason, bitter though it was. He should be at a hospital, she said to herself, but that was impossible. There was only this bed, hot water, and hope. She would not pray. That morning while she washed his body he looked like a child interrupted. There was innocence, promise, and waste. She cried for a man who could not cry back. She washed his hair, rubbed his wrinkles, scrubbed his chest's curly white hairs, and washed his feet. He lay on the bed, still. Maybe he too would rise on the third day. The Widow could only hope. She would not pray. At the window she saw the church and the Garvey house. Both rooftops were covered with John Crows.

On the evening of the second day, Lucinda wiped the Apostle from head to toe in warm water and soap. There was no need—his body smelt like incense—but Night Lucinda knew what she wanted. She had promised herself penance, so she gave herself over to abandon. Lucinda's prayers were not for the Apostle, but for herself. He lay on the bed like a Greek statue toppled from a page in his books. Lucinda had stayed in his room all this time.

She wiped him clinically at first, distributing soap evenly over his body, avoiding his phallus one minute, accidentally brushing it with her rag the next. The second wipe she did with care, using warm water, fearing that cold water would wake him. She ran the rag along his neck and felt his heat and pulse. There were spots on his body. Little red circles like the one below his lips. They were islands swimming in skin. From his chest to his thigh she used his spots to create a map, with a treasure chest in the center of his body. The Apostle groaned and Lucinda jumped, grabbed the rag and basin, and climbed off the bed. He was still unconscious. Were he to wake now, there would be no explanation. But perhaps there would be no need. Night Lucinda hissed; the sound of hunger. Her eyes explored the Apostle. His ruddy face hidden in his beard, the red scar below his lip, and his long arms. She would stare at his bushy chest hair and follow it right down to the center of him. When he tossed and his phallus swung pendulous, she touched herself.

Her mind was made up, the Widow would stop caring. But this was the third day and he was as still as the first. At times the Pastor would open his eyes as before, seeing nothing. She wondered what kind of calamity could have happened between the two men that would leave the church in shambles and the Rum Preacher unconscious. Outside, the road was still empty, save for the teasing wind and tormenting crows. She knew that Mr. Garvey did not meddle in poor people's affairs, but surely, she thought, he would bring back some order now. The man had the power of a massa, but perhaps the heart of one as well. Plus, he was the one who brought the Apostle here. She hoped the Apostle was dead even though she knew he wasn't. Hector Bligh was inside her. He was a stupid man, but his stupidity had infected her, causing her to give it new names, like devotion, passion, and mission. She knew nothing of spirits, but imagined the Preacher and the Apostle's battle a clash between Heaven and Hell, or maybe good and evil, but words like those meant nothing in Gibbeah. For a minute she imagined the Pastor as Superman in the movie serial that used to play at the Majestic. Perhaps Bligh was Superman and the Apostle a Super-Nazi-villain, and in their clash of super powers they laid the church to waste. Perhaps Bligh grabbed a bench all by himself and threw it at the Apostle, who dodged in time for it to crash into the altar. Then the Apostle would rip away a chunk of the wall and hurl it at the Preacher, who would punch the chunk to bits. Then both would fly into each other with a *Bang! Pow!* The thought made her chuckle. Then she looked at Bligh, motionless on the bed, and chuckled more. Her chuckle grew into a laugh, then a fit. As tears ran down her eyes, the Widow didn't know if she was laughing at grief or crying at laughter.

Since Lucinda wiped him last she had not dressed him. He was naked and she was naked too. And there was no shame. She was glad he was asleep.

On the third day the Widow awoke to the sound of scratching. She had slept in the living room, ignoring the mosquitoes. The scratching came from his room. John Crows. They had found a way in.

"Hector! Hector! Hect—"

On the left wall in the room, words curled and twisted, moving up and down and crossway in black and smudged gray. On the right wall, words circled a huge black cross like a whirlpool that spread from wall to window to floor. On the north wall, in front of the bed, came the sound of scratching. Bligh was writing words and numbers, crosses and hexes, and things she did not understand. His hair was wild and he wore only his white pants, which were covered in black smudges. Bligh wrote with fury, cutting into the wall, his hands moving faster than he could scribble. She looked away, at the ground, and saw her husband's papers, all scattered and covered with Bligh's writing. The sound of scratching cut through her.

"Hector?"

He wrote to the end of the wall and stopped. Turning around, their eyes met, but the Widow blinked first. Bligh approached her, dropping the pen from his hands. She saw through his eyes to a second face, one she had never seen before, one that filled her with a mighty fear. As he stepped toward her, she moved back, step for step.

"I thought they possessed him. You understand me?" he said, but not to her. "I thought he wanted to be exorcised from them but is them who want to be free from him."

"Hector?"

She stepped outside the doorway and only then saw the bottle standing in the window frame behind him. The cap was missing. Her husband drank rum from the same bottle the night before he died. The bottle she had hidden in the kitchen cupboard. Bligh closed the door.

Lucinda began to stroke him on the third day, this time without the excuse of soap and water. She discovered rivers and tributaries hidden between the hairs of his chest. Her fingers traveled southward and circled his navel, creating a whirlpool that disappeared inside his belly. As she pulled her fingers out of spin and inched toward his penis, the Apostle woke up. She jumped off the bed and ran to the corner of room marked off by shadow. Lucinda clutched her breasts and looked away, feeling his presence as he came back to life. The Apostle climbed off the bed and went toward her but saw his crucifix on the floor. As he bent to pick it up, she saw them. Spots, scars, red circles on his buttocks that looked like the red scar below his lip and on his chest and thighs.

"Lucinda," York said as he turned to her in the shadow, "what do you know about the tree of the knowledge of good and evil?"

THE HEALING

hey closed up the room to darkness and prepared the mirror. Lucinda had hesitated to carry out the Apostle's orders but she had no choice. The world had to know that the Rum Preacher could never defeat the Lord of Hosts. The world had to be told that the Apostle had been struck a mortal wound, but that wound had been healed. Lucinda was glad her church did not preach from the Book of Revelation, for this was a Revelation battle, something she had no wisdom for. The Apostle was as wise as Solomon. He read books of Solomon that were not in the Bible—so much wisdom that not even the greatest book could hold it all.

This was not what she saw in dreams. This was how her mother spoke in her thoughts. *Nasty nayga bitch, I can smell you fishy from here. You think is you him want? Who would a want a cross-eye, chi-chi blackatouch lacka you?*

In the room when he awoke, the Apostle stepped toward her and stopped so close that his chest hair touched her skin as he inhaled. She looked into his chest as he slung the crucifix around his neck. Lucinda yearned for his man-ness to rise and pierce her female-ness. Yes, she was a woman. Yes, she was beautiful. Yes, she was more than her mother. Between night and day was the real Lucinda, he would see. Her body would glow with the shock of dawn and drip with the wetness of dusk. Yes, this was a man, a father, not a papa who would leave. Yes, she would be devoted to the spirit, to him, praising his lordness and his magnificence. His hair, as it showered his sweaty face, and his manhood, that she would worship now, right now with her mouth. She stooped down, but he pulled her up.

"Lucinda." She had not looked at his face. If she had, he would not have broken her as he did. She would have heard her mother laugh as the prophecy came true.

"What the Hell are you doing? Lord forgive this, this whore of Babylon. Where are my . . . why are you . . . Father, forgive . . . Get out. And dress yourself, for pete's sake. Look here, between you and me? I just woke up. I should have my Five run you out of town, right now, but . . . even in this is love. Do you love me, Lucinda?

"Lucinda, do you love me?

"Lucinda?"

"Y-yes, Apostle."

"Then build my church. There are things you're going to have to do to make up for this gross, gross sin. Are you ready for penance?"

"Lucinda." His voice jolted her from memory. She was in his office, but had disappeared into her own space. "Leave us," he said.

The Apostle waved his fingers and she left him in the office with two of The Five, Brother Jakes, Brother Patrick.

"Bring him to me."

The rest came through the side door. Clarence refused to walk in step and had to be dragged along by Brother Vixton, the man who had whipped him, Tony Curtis, and Deacon Pinckney.

"Clarence, Clarence. What is this fight for? You think your hands long enough to box God? Sit down."

He refused, even though he limped and swayed and was close to collapse. The chair leapt out from the corner and knocked him behind the knees. Tony Curtis and Brother Vixton grabbed him just before he toppled over.

"I hear that you've been refusing to let people help you."

"I hear you did dead."

"Well, here I am, so whose report do you believe?"

"Him should a kill you."

"I'll let him know. Now, Clarence, don't you think that Mrs. Smithfield have better things to do than nurse wounds that you, you, Clarence, brought on yourself? You brought judgment on yourself, you know, Clarence, don't forget that. Look at me."

He refused at first but then his face felt strange. The Five were disturbed.

Just as Clarence's shoulders turned away from the Apostle, his head wrenched in the other direction. He strained against himself. Then his jaw betrayed him, following the twist of his neck. His face seemed to be tearing in two. Clarence gave up the fight.

"I said, look at me. There's nothing you can do, you know, Clarence, only One will reign supreme here."

The Apostle pulled up his chair in front of him and sat down.

"I'm concerned about you, my brother. You're not handling God's discipline well at all. What's this I hear about you pissing in Mrs. Smithfield's bed? About you spitting the soup back in her face? Imagine a big woman like her and a big man like you and she has to clean up your feces because you're too worthless to use the toilet. Worse, Clarence, worst of all, you won't let her treat your back. I can smell it rotting even now. Even now, puss is growing. But you don't care, do you? You think you're taking revenge on the Almighty. You think you'll just kill yourself and let him watch. You think you'll reject God's discipline, because that's what it was, you know, Clarence, God's discipline. And God disciplines those whom He loves. Do you think I love you, Clarence?

"Clarence, I asked you a question.

"Clarence, there are ways.

"Clarence, the Lord is growing tired of—"

The Apostle's nose was hit first. Phlegm that had been pooling in Clarence's mouth from nausea shot from his lips. Brother Vixton, needing no cue, struck Clarence in the back of his neck and he fell from the chair, yelling. The Apostle wiped his face.

"Pick him up."

Clarence struggled against The Five, strengthened by his insolence. Deacon Pinckney stuck a finger in his back and he yelled again. He released himself in their hands and was placed back on the chair.

"Clarence, I have forgiven you. You don't know what you do. Nor do you know what I could do to you." He leaned into Clarence and spoke softly. "There's still a side of your body that hasn't been whipped yet."

Clarence pulled back.

"There's no limit to what I will do for my Lord. You're breathing right now because of God's mercy and grace, because if it were up to me, I would beat the living daylights . . ." The Apostle raised his hand to strike and Clarence flinched, trembling.

"Look at you. You're like a dog afraid of his master." He leaned into Clarence again and whispered, "Are you ready to go to Hell? You think that once you get there you can come back? Well, my dear brother, you are certainly on that road. THIS IS WHAT DRAGGING YOU STRAIGHT TO HELL!"

The Five had not expected it either. They jumped along with Clarence, but the massive pain had struck him only, and he bowled over. Two of The Five held onto his arms. He could do nothing but bawl out loud. Tears wetted his lashes and flowed freely down his face. His scrotum was still in the Apostle's grip.

"God says that if your hand offends you, you should cut it off. What do you think I should do, Clarence?"

Clarence shook his head, trying to say no. The words formed in his mind, compounding on each other, each thought more panicked than the one before. But they failed to leave his mouth. He choked on himself.

"This is how I have you, Clarence. Right in the palm of my hand. Keep up with this sinful defiance and I'm going to forget myself and make a fist. Am I going to have problems with you?"

Clarence shook his head once more. He could only look with horror between his legs and between the Apostle's eyes. The Apostle had worked magic. He could not move.

"Good." The Apostle released his grip. "Leave us," he said to The Five. "Now. But turn on the light."

Clarence winced in the light as The Five left. When Brother Vixton shut the door, the sound jolted him and he gasped.

"Look at you. You think you're a man. But you're barely a boy. Look at you."

Clarence stared at the floor as he felt his muscles and limbs being freed. The pain in his belly was fading, but he clutched himself nonetheless. The Apostle stood up and put his hand on Clarence's head. "Clarence, the Lord has plans for you, but the Devil has plans for you too. Have you even once thought about what you have lost because of your weakness? You should have brought that weakness into the Kingdom. There's healing in the Kingdom, you know, Clarence. Miraculous healing."

Clarence felt an itch in the small of his back. Then the itch got worse, moving up in curves, slants, and darts. Something, one thing, many things, were moving all over his back. He thought he was going mad. They crawled up to the tip of his shoulder and went back down, traveling the well-grooved tears in his skin. The Apostle had cursed him with snakes. He tried to scream, but his mouth was dead again. He could not move. Clarence fell into spasms, his limbs frozen. The Apostle seemed sure. The snakes rubbed their scaly stomachs all over his back and under his shirt. He was petrified in the chair, his legs bolted to the floor. From his lips came the faint shape of the cry. The Apostle picked him up like paper and carried him over to the mirror.

"Miraculous healing, Clarence. Miraculous healing." Clarence tried to speak but the Apostle touched his lips and silenced him. York grabbed the tails of Clarence's shirt and pulled them up. He did not want to see snakes, but he could not move. The Apostle raised a hand mirror to Clarence's face and as he saw his back, his jaw fell. There were no snakes. His back was healing itself through the grooves of his wounds. The cuts closed like zippers and disappeared in the smoothness of his skin. He cried as his back left no trace of the whipping.

"Miraculous healing, Clarence. Do you want it?"

Clarence stared at his back in disbelief. The Apostle threw away the mirror.

"Follow me and I can lead you beyond pain, beyond sin, beyond miracles. I am the way, Clarence. I am the way. Beyond every single thing you thought about yourself. Beyond normal, beyond real. Every time you use this, this snake in your pants, you think you're killing the Devil inside you. You know of which Devil I speak. The Devil you've been trying to kill since you were twelve. The Devil in you that was stealing looks between my legs just now when I was sitting in front of you. You'll never kill it. Not through pain, not through sin. No matter how many times you come inside a woman, you'll never kill your heart's real desire."

The Apostle touched Clarence's crotch again, but this time he did not make a fist.

"Lucinda, tell them to go to the Johnson's house," the Apostle said while peering from the cracked door. "Oh, and Lucinda, tell them to carry cutlasses."

When The Five got to the Johnson's, the door was already open. Inside was dark, with the doorway at the back of the house an oblong of light. They passed through the house and followed the light outside. On the bottom step was Mrs. Johnson, her back bleeding and her arms wrapped around herself. She rocked back and forth, humming what sounded like a hymn. The breeze whispered through the trees, and looking up, they saw the reason for the cutlass. Swinging from a rope that hung from a high branch was Mr. Johnson, dressed for combat in his camouflage uniform from the World War. His arms were still and his neck was squeezed tight in a noose. At the foot of the tree, a blue stool was toppled over. The breeze whispered again and his body swung, agreeing.

JUBILEE

Church was full. At 8:30 at night there was no moon. Most came because of the miracle. The Rum Preacher had killed the Apostle, they said. He was dead, but then he came back on the third day, Lucinda would testify. She could do no less, the man was within her. Down the road, the Widow's house merged with the darkness. No candle was lit. The Widow had not seen the Rum Preacher since the day he woke up. He had bolted his door from the inside.

The organist played one hymn on the battered instrument. This was no time for praise and worship, the word was too crucial tonight. Nobody could get a hint out of Lucinda, or The Five. Secrets seemed to brim in Clarence, a surprise to most. He seemed to have received a miracle himself even though he would not testify. Clarence was on the pulpit, somewhere Lucinda was never allowed, and this struck many as most curious. He was dressed in Sunday clothes, his black suit and gray shirt with tan buttons that matched his skin. But he was a distraction, not who they'd come to see.

And there he was. Nobody saw him emerge. His black and red robes billowed though there was no wind. His hair was brushed back off his face. He spread his arms wide and the organist played a flourish.

"Hallelujah! Hallelujah!"

"Consuming fire! Consuming fire!"

"Praise the Lord."

"Saints," York shouted, "I've come back to you! The Devil came to steal, kill, and destroy, but *No!* Say it after me . . . *No!*"

"NO!"

"NO!"

"That's what I told the Devil in the pit of darkness. I told him I reject the death from sin and embrace the life of the Father. The abomination tried to snuff out the faithful, but Praise the Lord, I'm still here! I'm still here! I'm still here.

"And so are you. But oh, did he try to smite your Apostle. Oh sacara-janga-hosepha, did he and his demons try to slay your appointed one. And he did, but by grace of God, I just beat him back. Vixton, you should have seen me. I just go so . . . batter him with the shield of faith, then I buck him with the helmet of salvation, then you know what I do next? You know what I do? I just slay him with the sword of the spirit."

"Hallelujah!"

"Praise the Lord!"

"Consuming fire!"

"Sicorsa-rakatok!"

"But—" the Apostle said softly.

"Praise the—"

"I said BUT! He slayed me too. But praise the Lord. Where is the Preacher now, eh? Death, where is your sting?"

"Hallelujah!"

"Praise the Lord!"

"Now listen to me carefully. When I was sleeping the Lord showed me new things. New revelation like John. Gibbeah, I told you that this is war. We are fighting war. Every man and woman must put on the armor. Who ready to slay for the Lord? Who ready to usher in the Kingdom? The Lord showed me when I was dead. It's time for Gibbeah to get serious or it shall perish."

"No, Apostle, no!"

"Our Father in Heaven—"

"Who here want to perish? Who here really want to roast in the lake of fire, eh? That is where Gibbeah heading. That is where you heading tonight if you don't come back to the Lord. I said it before and I'll say it again. If your hand offends, you cut it off. If you eye seeing sin, cut it out! Cut it out! Cut it out! Oh, I know I preaching to somebody tonight, Hallelujah.

"Gibbeah, the Lord is vengeful but He is also merciful. We can have Heaven right here on Earth. Wouldn't you like to have Heaven on Earth, Mrs. Fracas? Who don't want Paradise, raise your hand. What if I told you that God has shown me how Gibbeah can have Paradise? Do you want Paradise? You, Mrs. Smithfield, do you want Paradise? You at the back, how about you? My ladies at the front, do you want Paradise?"

"Hallelujah!"

"Well, you can have Paradise. God is going to give Heaven to you. God is going to give it to you tonight. But you must be ready. Tonight I'm going to show you how to get ready. Touch the person beside you and say get ready. Now touch them and say the Lord is in this house. Good. Good.

"Good. Get ready. The first thing we're going to do is kill all distraction in Gibbeah. So from tonight we having worship every night. Touch the person beside you and say every night. From tonight I don't want any family to sit together. I don't want brother beside sister, I don't want husband beside wife. I don't want anybody distracted from God's work by carnal things. I don't want anybody distracted by which rent to pay and which child need a spanking. Besides, everybody in this church is a brother or a sister, we are all family.

"I expect everybody in church, every night. God doesn't care if you're sick. Come to the church and get healing, Hallelujah. Some nights I want the men alone to worship as brothers and some nights I want the women alone to worship as sisters. And I said it before and I'll say it again. The Devil is prowling like a roaring lion, looking for people to devour. I don't want to see any strange face in Gibbeah again. The next person to cross that bridge will be the Devil in disguise, mark my word. And if we let the Devil pass, you'll have a lot more than two calves to deal with. You know who the Devil coming for? Your babies. He's gunning for you like a German tank. He's seen the good that the Lord is doing and wants to snatch it for himself. But what do we say when the Devil come to steal? What do we say? I'm not hearing you? That's right. NO!

"You have all seen the miracles. You have all seen the signs and wonders. You have seen the resurrection. That's because I am the resurrection.

"I am the resurrection! I am the vicar of God. Nobody can come to Him unless through me. I saved you from witchcraft. I broke the curse on Gibbeah. I banished all demons back to Hell. The Loooooord is in my hands. Look and tremble!"

LEVITICUS

Riddle we this and riddle we that. Guess we this riddle or perhaps not. Jack Sprat could eat no fat. So the Devil come take him and that was that.

So who judgment goin fall pon next?

Who?

Pon who judgment goin fall?

Who?

Could a be she, could a you.

No true.

If not she, then a who?

You?

Judgment fall pon the Majestic where nuff sin did show. Judgment come with fire and brimstone and now we not goin have no more Devil picture show. Satan come like a roaring lion, but God roar louder and Majestic fall in fire.

Judge them two by two.

Who?

Judge them two by two.

Judgment come from the white throne. Judgment fall pon Mr. and Mrs. Johnson. She the whore of Babylon who get discipline right. Now her back have scar like spider web.

She give up the pokie to another man.

Soil the marriage bed with adultery.

She goin burn in Hell where them goin shove pitchfork in her pokie.

Hallelujah, praise the Almighty, cause Him judge with fury. And her husband dead like Judas. The Lord is vengeful but the Lord is merciful. Clarence get vengeance, then him get mercy.

Clarence and the Apostle, closer than a brother.

Two is two is two.

Judgment fall pon the Contraptionist long before. Him cocky turn friend with cow pokie. Judgment come down with lightning and thunder. Leviticus Twenty, verse fifteen.

Judgment fall pon Massa Fergie. The Contraptionist partner in sinnery. By their fruit we know who them be. Lightning expose him sinnery. If a man lie with beast, he shall surely be put to death.

And ye shall slay the beast.

One man deh with cow, then two.

Judge them two by two.

Judgment goin fall pon them who did take seat with the Rum Preacher.

Them was six, and six is three times two.

Judge them two by two.

Judgment goin fall pon the Rum Preacher and the Widow whore. Them in the house doin sin. Them in the house taking order from Beelzebub. The white throne of judgment goin crash pon them roof. It goin smash everything asunder.

Judgment goin come pon the Rum Preacher for all iniquity that him bring with him. Judgment goin come for what him do to the Apostle.

The Rum Preacher strike and kill the Apostle. But the Apostle rise after three day. Evil get beat by good, black get beat by white. The Apostle is the way, the truth, and the light. The Lord goin send signs and wonders. The Lord goin exalt the Apostle and put him on the right hand of God. The Rum Preacher goin be wailing with gnashing of teeth.

And the Widow too.

Judge them two by two.

But the biggest judgment that ever goin fall, goin fall on the black house. The house of Sodom where Gibbeah pitch tent. The house of sin where rivers of damnation flow. Is through him that all sin come. From in him and out him, all sin be.

The one them call Mr. Garvey.

Fire pon him cause him fuck batty.

Fire pon him cause him think him better than we.

Fire pon him because it easier for a camel to go through the eye of a needle than for a rich man to enter the Kingdom of God.

The Lord have judgment for the rich too.

Is not we to judge, not me not you.

We no know what a go on. The Apostle don't say nothing bout that house yet.

But sin must come from it or the house wouldn't be black.

See them John Crows how them line up on him roof.

Judgment coming to smite the house down.

The John Crow know.

Him have six nephew who don't look like him.

And them never grow up, what a thing.

Man mustn raise boy, is mother them need.

Him sin like Onan and throw way him seed.

But is rich man things, so make we see what God goin do.

When judgment come pon him, judgment goin come true.

Judge the sodomite and the Rum Preacher.

Judge them two by two.

So who judgment goin fall pon next?

Who?

Pon who judgment goin fall?

Who?

Could a be me, could a you.

CLOVEN FEET

The Apostle made a proclamation for the extermination of all bovines by axe and fire. Since nobody understood the proclamation, including Clarence who went to the crossroads to proclaim it, the Apostle issued another one. All cows and goats were to be slaughtered and burnt before Sunday; swine would be spared. The first was a stubborn kill, a bull whose life and will were as joined as sin and consequence, Sodom and Gomorrah. The bull had seen enough of humans to pay them no heed, but snorted when he caught the murderous glimmer of cutlasses and axes. The first took a swing, missed, turned to run, and was gored straight up the ass, then tossed like an old flower. The second struck as a midnight thief, chopping off the tail and crippling its balance. Another struck the bull's left hind leg and he collapsed. Chops fell upon the bull like rain.

The Widow left his door alone. She had sat facing it all night, falling asleep in her armchair and waking as her chin struck her chest. She stared at the door's deep blue through the haze of her barely awake eyes and thought of the Rum Preacher who probably hadn't slept. He would be writing on the floor even now, or perhaps on his skin. There was no coming back—he was mad as Hell. But he was hers now and she felt like a mother and a lover whenever she allowed herself to. Most times the Widow reached for a cynicism and scorn that she could barely conjure. She tried to hate but hate came out as pity, she spoke a curse but curse came out as prayer. He was inside her. She hated him, she thought, as all women must hate the men who undid them. Who was he, this bastard who came into her house with so little and now had even less? But that less included her heart, even though she would never admit such a thing. A man who lost his mind was like one who lost his life; unable to hurt or promise. But he had hurt her. Pain came in waves through the promise of the light blue door. Was he writing about her? Outside, children awoke to the scream of goats.

She made him breakfast, knowing it would be left uneaten and waited until 11 o'clock. The Widow Greenfield was going to see the Apostle. She knew he was strong where Bligh was weak, so maybe he would listen to her plea. She ignored the trees and wind that whispered her folly. The street was empty, but at the church doorway, as if waiting, was Lucinda.

"Me is here to see York."

"Apostle to you."

"Me is here to see him."

"What a thing. What make you think him want to see you? Is the whore of Babylon you is, him say so himself."

"Me no come her fi quarrel with you."

"Then hi, what you come here for, fi labrish? Come make me lap frock tail and we can sit down and correspondence." As Lucinda stood in her way with her arms akimbo, the Widow remembered the last time they were this close. Long before Lucinda showed up in the rain to tell her that Bligh was invited back to church. Long before the Widow became a wife and Lucinda became a Sister.

It was shortly before the Widow got married, when she warned Lucinda to stay away from her husband-to-be by punching her in the face. Lucinda had found herself in love with Mr. Greenfield after he had fucked her and left her down by the river. Back then she vowed that over her dead body was Mary Palmer, her enemy since childhood, going to marry her man. Lucinda would lay in bed clutching a pillow and ramming herself with a green banana as she imagined Mr. Greenfield wetting her with his sweat. He was going to marry Mary over her dead body. The Widow had heard the rumors, most started by Lucinda herself. *"How him moo like cow when him cocky ready fi shoot and how him cocky bent but big."* Then there were rumors that he would buy Mary's house from Mr. Garvey and give it to Lucinda. Hearsay would have been enough were it not for Lucinda showing up wherever they went, laughing out loud at Mr. Greenfield's jokes and sighing at how great a boyfriend he was. Gibbeah didn't know what to think, especially when word spread that it was Lucinda, not Mary, who was going to be married. Lucinda's mother, seeing the disgrace her daughter was bringing upon her name, followed her as she followed the couple to the grocery. She grabbed Lucinda by the hair and dragged her home, beating her all the way. The next week her mother was dead, drowned in the Two Virgins River, with Lucinda's foot pinning her head underwater. Lucinda, who had waited all her life to cream her hair, told the hairdresser that she needed a hairdo for both a funeral and a wedding.

Lucinda remembered that day, sitting in the hairdresser's chair as Mary stomped toward her. Maybe she said, *Cross-eye chi-chi, leave me man,* maybe she didn't. Lucinda remembered thinking that only spirits could move so fast. She remembered Mary's fist speeding toward her face. The rest was dark, like the swollen circle around her eye that throbbed when she touched it.

Both women remembered the last time they were so close and both now realized that the power had shifted. Lucinda raised her chin and looked down at the Widow.

"The Apostle don't have no business with iniquity lacka you."

"The Apostle can speak for himself, Lucinda." The Widow saw his face and felt hope and distress. Coming toward them was Clarence, handsome as always, his eyes puffy from having awakened not long before. Both women knew that those clothes weren't his. The Widow glared at Lucinda as she stepped past her and followed Clarence inside the church. Walking down an aisle that felt foreign even before the Apostle came, the Widow hoped that this was the same Clarence, the man she held an affection for despite his relentless attempts, when they were young, to force himself between her and her panties. But Clarence stepped with purpose, a determination that seemed reinforced by his silence. This was not the Clarence she knew. There was no hope in his stride. He left her at the door.

Hearing no call, she went in. He was at the desk writing in a big red book that looked like a Bible. "Well, what is it I can do for the Widow woman?" he said. The Widow read his tone as mockery. She looked left and right, fearing The Five at any second. "Well?"

"Mista York."

"I prefer Apostle."

"Apostle. Apostle York. I . . ."

"You . . ."

"I was—"

"You were—"

"I was—"

"Either you're about to say something or you're not. Which is it?"

"Is about the Preacher."

"That malignant spot on the church's backside. What about him? Is he well? Is he asleep? Is he in bed? Has that Devil recovered from trying to kill me?"

"Him . . ."

"He's . . . well, out with it, woman, you can't make sentences out of just one word. What are you trying to say to me? Are you trying to ask me something?"

"I know you stronger and him weaker."

"Yes, God has made my strength perfect in his weakness. It was written, anyway. Children of darkness have no power over the child of light. He will not . . ."

"Leave him be."

"Pardon me?"

"Leave him be. Me asking you to leave him be."

"What is his welfare to you? Oh, I see."

"I, I didn't say nothing."

"Yes you did, every fidget said more than words. Bligh seems to be doing more in his bed than just sleeping."

"No! We not into nothing."

"Then what is your business with him? You did your good deed, somebody had to. Now is the time to leave him to God's judgment or God's mercy, who knows."

"But Mista Y—"

"Apostle."

"Apostle. Him feeble, you know. Him feeble bad. Him can't do you nothing. Him can't even wipe him batty. Pastor Bligh can't bother you no more. Him can't even do nothing for himself. Just leave him be. I . . . I feel sorry him."

"You feel sorry for a stray dog, but I don't hear no barking coming from your bedroom. Maybe I should be listening for something else."

"No sinning happening in me house."

"We all sin, Mary. That's what makes redemption sweeter."

"Just leave him be."

"No can do. You know what *no can do* means? Of course not, your negro head has never been to a Kingston school. It means, what you ask is out of the question. What God has begun He will see through to its completion. There's no hope for Hector Bligh. But there may be for you."

"What you say?"

"You heard me. Look, this is what the Lord is saying. Turn him over. Now, right now. Go home and turn him out. Drag him out, kick him out, push him out, lead him out like the Pied Piper. Hand him over to me."

She watched him as he rose, looked at her as if to approach, and sat down again. "No," she said, and turned to leave.

"Don't condemn yourself to Hell along with him. I'm giving you a chance for life, and life more abundant. Turn him over now."

"No." The last time the Apostle wanted Bligh, she thought, he had sent his men to get him. But now he was asking her to hand him over.

"You wouldn't be asking me for him if you could get him yourself."

"I can bring Hellfire down on that damn house right now! Where are you going? How dare you step away from me, you whore. Clarence!"

She dashed past Clarence and Lucinda and ran toward her house.

"Clarence!" the Apostle shouted again. Both he and Lucinda ran to the office, but as Clarence stepped in, he shut the door in her face.

The Widow bolted her front door. Hector Bligh was still in his room. The knowledge gave her something she would never admit to be reassurance. God was working through him and he was working through her. She sat in front of the door and waited. She waited for Him, she waited for The Five, she waited for the Apostle and the Devil.

AN AROMA

L ucinda went inside her house and shut the door tight. She lit a candle, but when the shadows began to dance before her, blew it out. At church, Clarence had shut the door in her face, hitting her nose. Lucinda was furious. She had the Apostle first. She prepared the way. She was his John the Baptist, Clarence was merely a Magdalene with a penis. She was disturbed to see them together. His beauty matched the Apostle's and they looked like brothers, partners, or angels joined at the hip. She thought that there must have been something in her that now displeased him or made this man please him more. Day Lucinda whispered about her smell. How had she not smelt herself before? The aroma that tainted her. The smell of tea that he knew she drank. What did he want? He asked her to be pious, then he asked her to speak chants. He wanted her for God, he wanted her for Sasa, now he didn't want her at all. He held her close, but gave her no secrets. She was still his helper, but felt outside his purpose. Perhaps he wanted beauty, which she did not have. He held her at bay like a cherished but smelly thing.

But she would enter his most holy place; Lucinda was determined. She would tear down the curtains as red as the bold red tip of his—no, she would not think of such things. The Apostle wanted a different kind of worship. Something Clarence seemed to understand already. No matter. She would do better than that pretty but stupid man who could never do arithmetic. She would get rid of the smell.

Vinegar. The sour jars that kept lizard skins and dog paws. She threw them away but the smell remained. She came to realize that the smell was a presence that was everywhere. In the flame of the candle she relit. In the soft sound of dew falling, the shrill cries of cicadas, and the little lights of fireflies dancing around her like tiny stars. The presence was in her secrets. The presence knew that even in day there was night in her heart that was black as tar.

"Me don't know how it happen, Apostle," Lucinda said. "One minute me cooking the dinner, next thing me know, whoom! Fire bursting out from everywhere!"

"Fire bursting out from everywhere. I see."

"Is all me could a do fi save meself. Is the Devil."

"I'm sure."

"Me don't have nowhere to live now."

"But that's not true, Lucinda. The fire didn't burn down the house. I hear that the walls are still standing."

"But me can't go back there. Everything burn up. Me no even have no bed to rest me tired body."

"I'm sure there's a friend more than willing."

"Me no have no friend. Everybody jealous o me. Oh Lord, see me dying trial. Is woe deh pon me. How me going to make it through, woi, Puppa Je—"

"Lucinda, enough! I will instruct the people."

"You have a bedroom up in the steeple."

"What? In the steeple? How do you know this? I've never heard about a room? Clarence, you know about this?"

"No. Plus, even if one up there, it must be full of dirt and cobweb."

She noticed that he did not say "Apostle" or "sir" after "no."

"No, it did clean," she said. "Me did clean it before you come."

They stood in silence as the Apostle made up his mind. She looked at Clarence and felt victory. He went over to the Apostle by the window and whispered. She saw their shoulders touch. "Alright, Lucinda, you can have the room until you sort out your business."

"*Thank you, Jesus,*" she whispered. She wanted to glare at Clarence, but his back was to her as he said something quietly to the Apostle again.

Midnight had come, but she could not sleep. She was higher now, higher than everybody in the village. From her window she could see everything. The dirty rooftops stained by fallen mangos. The lonely orange light in the

Widow's window, the very end of Brillo Road, and behind her, the Apostle's quarters. She had watched all night. Clarence did not leave.

BANG

The next morning, the Apostle gave the church spiritual armor. It came from the Book of Mark:

And when ye hear of wars and rumors of wars, be ye not troubled: for such things must needs be; but the end shall not be yet.

For nation shall rise against nation, and kingdom against kingdom: and there shall be earthquakes in diverse places, and there shall be famines and troubles: These are the beginnings of sorrows.

The sun shall be darkened and the moon not give her light, and the stars of Heaven shall fall and the powers that are in Heaven shall be shaken.

And then they shall see the Son of Man coming in the clouds with great power and glory. And then He shall send His angels and shall gather together his elect from the four winds, from the uttermost part of the Earth to the uttermost part of Heaven.

He told them he had come from the clouds in this, the end of days. God was rocking the very ground and shaking strongholds loose. Now was time to enter the ark. Gibbeah was the ark, already perfectly built by God to be surrounded by a river with only the bridge connecting it to weakness and evil. Every heart in Gibbeah was pure, save two. Those two. Satan's emissary and the whore of Babylon. If action wasn't taken soon, the enemy's foothold would turn into a stronghold. Nine days ago, the Rum Preacher, that foot sol-dier of Hell, had tried to kill him, but evil could never triumph over good. In the twinkling of an eye, the Sodom cinema fell to judgment. God had judged with consuming fire.

Go down Emmanuel Road
Gal an boy
Fi go broke rock-stone
Broke them one by one
Gal an boy
Finger mash don't cry
Gal an boy
Remember a play we deh play

Monday morning come and we waiting for the truck. Is the Lord goin take over now. We waiting with purpose for the Lord give we power. The Apostle give we the sword of the spirit. Him say only evil coming over that bridge, so we stand.

So we wait.

Then it come.

The truck humming and bumming and shaking up the road like earthquake. Yellow and red like the Devil. But we ready. We goin in the enemy camp and take back what he stole. Is not a truck, is a ship from Hell.

Hell.

Hell.

Hell.

The demon come out of the truck and a smile with we like we give him joke. We give him something else. Brother Jakes grab a stone first. We didn't talk. As the driver open the door and jump out we start pick up stone. The first stone lick him and nearly knock him out and him left eye explode with blood. Him bawl out and manage to climb back in the truck, but not before we buss him head-back and clap him in him shoulder, back, batty, and seed bag.

Damn demon. Him scream. We break him windshield and the two side window. Even the little pickney know how to deal with demon. Him back up the truck and him lick down somebody then drive over him. Nobody never scream or nothing, cause we know say that boy did do God work so is Heaven him gone straight to. The truck screech and speed off, with stone raining pon the roof with a *Bup! Bup! Bang!*

Those who had rebelled against the church by pitching tent with Pastor Bligh repented of their sin. They also repented of witchcraft, Devilry, horoscope, bearing false witness, chocolate, perversion, fornication, bestiality, incest, dancing, music listening, wearing short dresses, and washing one's pokie or cocky too long in the bathtub—anything to make the whipping shorter. The Apostle was firm: Evil had to be driven out. When they cut the youngest and weakest of the sinners loose from the whipping tree, she fell to the ground and did not rise. Anybody who felt to question the Apostle feared The Five after that.

TONIGHT

Clarence pulled off the left shoe first, then the right. He cradled the Apostle's right foot in his palm and tugged the black sock slowly. The robes were tossed to one side of the bathroom with the other dirty laundry for Lucinda to wash the next day. Clarence heard music in his head, a slow song, a foreign one crooned by a white man. He looked up and saw the Apostle's face. The bathroom was in brilliant light. Clarence pulled the Apostle's belt buckle and the pants fell. He shut his eyes.

York's hands were on his shoulders, squeezing. Clarence expected a man's squeeze, not soft, and the Apostle held him firm. But then he squeezed tighter. He grabbed tighter still, digging his fingers into Clarence's shoulders as if to pull the bones out. Clarence looked up in shock. The Apostle grunted, his eyes rolled back, and his head jerked.

"Apostle?" Clarence whimpered, trying to pry the hands off his shoulders. The Apostle was yelling now and he shuddered and swayed as if having a drunken fit. Clarence pulled his grip loose and the Apostle staggered, falling into the bath.

"Apostle!"

The shower curtain popped away from its hinges one by one. Water burst from the tap. The Apostle bellowed. Clarence froze.

"Apostle?"

"It's him! Abba babbaha ricocasrabotok!"

"Apos—"

"It's him, ricocasrabotok! He's attacking me! From that goddamn house, the son of a bitch is attacking me! Aahhh!"

"Who? Who attacking?"

"*Him*, you fucking imbecile! Bligh! Bligh!" The shower erupted but York raised two fingers and the water stopped. He was out of breath yet climbed out. Clarence reached to help him and was pushed away. Clarence tried again.

"Get the fuck away from me!"

Clarence felt a punch to his chest that sent him slamming against the door. But the Apostle had not touched him; York was rubbing his scalp.

"Get my Five. Get them now. It ends tonight, goddamn. Tonight! Get me my Five! I want that fucking bastard dead right now, so help me! Right now!"

The Widow's yard was ridden with carrion; stinking vulture flesh and scattered feathers. Somehow, whenever a John Crow landed on her grass it fell immediately to its death. Or perhaps crow had begun to eat crow. From her window she had seen them fall. She looked behind her to Bligh's closed door and wondered if he was writing on the wall still. There was a rumble and the window shook suddenly. All the John Crows that waited on Mr. Garvey's roof took off at once. She turned her gaze to the gate and there they were.

Men and women, some of whom she had known all her life. Some who were neither friend nor enemy. They were all in front of her gate, side by side in a perfect line. At first they were silent and seemed not to blink. Then the throng parted and Brother Vixton came to the front, stroking his whip like an extension of himself. Much younger than the Widow, he waved his youth like his whip. He was the tallest of The Five and he lumbered like a field slave having won freedom and purpose. He saw her.

"Unu remember what Proverbs Seven say?

"Unu remember what Proverbs Seven say?

"Me say if unu remember what Proverbs Seven say?"

Brother Vixton turned his back to the Widow and scolded the crowd. He raised his whip high and they staggered back, some tripping over people who fell behind them.

> Hearken unto me now therefore, O ye children,
> and attend to the words of my mouth
> let not thine heart decline to her ways

go not astray in her paths
for she has cast down man wounded
yea, many a strong man have been slain by her
Her house is the way to Hell, going down
To the chambers of death.

"This a the house! This a the house!"

The mighty man of God made one mighty step onto the Widow's lawn and fell, first on his knees, then on his face, and his eyes went white. The ground shook like Jericho. The whip flew out of his hand and landed in the road like a dead snake. Men and women scattered, some screaming. From Brother Vixton's eyes, nose, ears, and mouth sprung black blood. The Widow turned away. She was neither frightened nor saddened, but shivered and wept nevertheless. Below the window she collapsed, falling asleep.

The Widow dreamt of dead men who swung from whips that turned into snakes, scepters, and maypoles, which then spun off several shards of red that turned into knives that shot off in all directions, killing the first born. She awoke.

Outside, Brother Vixton's body was shiny from dew. The night had the stillness of a painting, which may be why at first the Apostle blended in. She blinked several times and still he was real, and he looked at her, his robes blowing even though there was no wind. Everything in her wanted to run, except her feet, which were planted by the window. York's face was the only thing that was not black with the night, so when he turned away his hair bled into the dark and he vanished.

THE BLACK HOUSE

not until sundown did the Widow gain courage to step. Nobody had passed by her house since the night before. Another voice, one that she had never heard, told the Widow that no harm would come to her on the grass. Maybe it was the Lord, maybe the Rum Preacher, who had stopped speaking in words but perhaps in thoughts and dreams. The cold, dewy grass slid through her slippers and chilled her feet. As she stepped over John Crows, the Widow's fear threatened to overtake her. She would kick a bird and it would scream, rising fully formed and malevolent. She stepped wide of Brother Vixton, fearing that the evil spirits that entered him could still cause his body to wake up. Maybe he was not dead or asleep. Maybe he was awake and waiting for her to come close so that he could rip her head off and drink blood from her neck. She stepped wide. The road was empty. Sometimes night church went on until late morning. With cutlass in hand she was ready.

Nobody had seen Mr. Garvey in a very long time. No face looked out from Mr. Garvey's window, no sound came from his door. His nephews seemed to have all grown up and left. But there were nights when a faint light shone through the door cracks and windowsills. *Him think him too good for black people. Him don't mix.* But the village was his. He owned every red building including the church. Surely he could drive the Apostle out of the village and put Gibbeah back where it used to be. She thought for a minute about what that meant. Hypocrisy was as much a shield for her as anybody else. Pretense was protection. The Widow pulled the gate, hoping that she was right and that the dogs were dead. She nearly tripped scrambling up the steps.

"Mr. Garvey? Mr. Garvey? Mr. Garvey, sir? Mr. Ga—" She threw herself down on the verandah floor. Two lanterns passed each other in the dark, bidding good night, praise the Lord, don't be late cause the Apostle have a word bout last night. The lanterns swirled out of sight and the voices out of earshot. Guarding the door was another door with a wooden frame, covered in a tight mosquito mesh like the doors of dusty houses in John Wayne movies. She knocked and whispered his name. The night sucked out her sound.

"Mr. Garvey, Mr. Garvey, sir? Mr. Garvey?" she hissed. The cutlass shone in the dark and taunted her. As if she could kill *anybody*. The darkness was stealing her hope. She thought of the man in her dead husband's room scrawling the last lines of his sanity on the ceiling.

The Widow called Mr. Garvey one last time. In a disappointed silence she turned to leave. She swung the cutlass stronger than intended and hit the door, which swung open a few inches and grated against the rust caked up in the hinges. Curious and desperate, she stepped past the first and found the second door unlocked as well. Before she let herself in, a stench confronted her, an odor far more overwhelming than the one locked up in her house. An odor that was all around her but nowhere near; just like God, she thought. Age, offal, and decay. Things that would weaken a woman. In the dark, the room felt hot and damp. The Widow stepped inside and tripped over something hard and soft, like a tough lump in a carpet. She should have carried a candle. But then she would have been seen. There she was in darkness, blind as a bat. She moved north, unsure why, and tripped again, hissing. Since the Rum Preacher came into her house, she had been wearing blue again. She had also stopped cussing.

The room reeked of spoiled meat. She knew full well the cruel joke of dead flesh. How the stench always crept up like a fragrance only to molest her with putrefaction lying beneath. It was the scent of pork left out too long or a dead batch of baby rats. Mr. Garvey's refrigerator was closed, but the kitchen window was open. The sounds of church came into the room. She pulled the black curtain to cover the window. This was the kitchen, which meant stove, which meant matches. The pink tip burst into flame and sulphur burnt her nostrils. Light swamped the kitchen, covering the white Formica counter in a sheet of orange. Shadows in the corners of the room danced with the flickering flame. She found candles in the cupboard under the double sink.

"Mr. Garvey?" The living room was in the center of the house. Furniture was tossed out of place. Danger hung like a ghost between upturned chairs and tables. The candle winked each time it passed a broken mirror or painting. There were shattered cups, plates, and bottles on the floor. The smell of piss came from everywhere.

"Mr. Garvey?" The Widow had left the living room, following the candle-light upstairs and down a narrow hallway. The house seemed to be getting smaller. She refused to open doors that were already closed. This was as far as she had gone into anybody's house. She thought herself no different than the John Crows or Brother Vixton who lay dead on her lawn, two who paid the price for the sin of trespass. But she had come too far and he was her only hope, even if he was a sodomite. The Widow had her opinions about old bachelors, especially those who were well-raised, rich, and still woman-less. But to each his own, she sighed; Mr. Garvey wasn't the only pervert in Gibbeah. The inseparable Scottforth twins who no longer lived in the village had separated when both tried to marry the same goat. In all her life she had known men only at their point of brokenness. The Widow protected herself with bitterness so that no man could disappoint her. To her, men had their use but they were not actually men at all. Only boys who got bigger, taller, and longer, if they were lucky. But men were broken in a way that no woman could fix. The only full man was a dead one, because that was the only time mind and body did the same thing. The corridor seemed to stretch longer.

She closed in on herself, pulling her arms tighter and hiding her neck in the hunch of her shoulders. The last door was shut but the one before was open, if only slightly.

Mr. Garvey had his back to her. She could never sit facing a window in her house as he did, his back facing the open front door. Her house was her mother's, then her husband's, and never felt like hers, not even after he died. How different a house must feel to the owner. On every wall would be the mark of possibility. He could do any damn thing he wanted, including nothing. He could let the house fall to ruin or blow a hole in the side wide enough for a cloud to slip in. Or he could let the house become a big toilet as Mr. Garvey had done. Then he could sit, face to the window, back to the door, as if no demon dare sneak up to him in his own kingdom.

The dark blue curtains were pulled back and through the window she saw stars. This was the rear of the house that was away from the road but close to the river. Mr. Garvey could see in the dark. Eyes like his could see through the night, the curtain, the window, and even the walls that enclosed him. From behind the huge, dark armchair she could see the tip of his head, crowned with thinning hair.

"Mr. Garvey? Mr.—Mr. Garvey? Is me, sir. I mean, is Mrs. Greenfield. I don't know if you remember me or anything. Me is Miss Palmer daughter? You remember Miss Palmer? She dead long time now and—oh Lord Jesus, you must a wonder why this mad woman barging into you house this time o night, but Mr. Garvey, you don't see what goin on in the place? You don't see how the Devil taking over Gibbeah? You don't see how people taking liberty with you land like say them own it? All sort of obeahism and Devilism and this new preacher, you don't see what him turning people into? Mr. Garvey?"

Mr. Garvey did not answer. He remained still, his back and the back of the chair to her. She felt rejected by the wall of his snobbery. It made her angrier and bolder.

"You know something, Mr. Garvey? Me know that you no care too much bout black people, but is not like say me asking you for nothing. After all, my husband buy fi him house, we don't rent from you. But at least you should a care bout Mrs. Johnson house that them burn down—nuh your house that? And what happen to the cinema? You just going make all these things happen?" She was right behind him, almost touching the back of his indifference.

"Mr. Garvey, is you me talking to, you know, me know say you no deaf. Or is only brown boy mouth you hear? You think me business if you want your little idiot town to go to hell? You think me care?" She grabbed the back of the armchair.

"Is you me talking to, you stringy-hair little sodomite!" She shook the chair. His head popped off, rolled down his neck, bounced into his lap, fell to the floor, and spun until stopped by the wall below the window. From his neck came bugs, flies, and a horrendous stench. Between bone, flesh still moved, but candlelight revealed the movement to be maggots. She grabbed her mouth and screamed into the palm of her hand, but did not run. As the Widow remembered all the dead people she had seen in her life, she felt a calm that was strange even to her. She remembered Brother Vixton and the trickle of black blood that fled from his nostrils, and felt calmer still. A dead man was unable to hurt or promise.

The way Mr. Garvey cradled the things in his lap she would never have guessed them to be his genitals. But there was more. His eyes were gone and insects fed on his wetter parts. At first she thought his head had broken off from rot, but his neck was cut jagged and sharp in a butcher's way. She turned away, looked under the desk beside him, and under the desk looked back at her.

He was barely a boy and he stunk as well. His eyes were craters, nothing but hollow circles of darkness, but they saw her. His skin had sunken onto bone and looked wrinkled, even in the silvery light. She ran from the room, feeling a heaviness that she could not understand nor bear. In the room two doors down was another body. He was bent over on the bed, the way she would be bent over by her husband whenever he wanted to see her vagina but not her face. She looked at the body and felt a similar coldness. The busy buzz of insects drew her to his back that was chopped into grooves, and his neck that was missing a head. She ran and tripped, her hand clutching the softness of fabric and flesh tearing away too easily. There were two, the first older, though still a youth, and the other a boy who seemed feminine. Maybe it was his pose, one final defiant act of effeminate grace. Bits of paper had stuck to his cheek. In the dark she could see that they were photographs, but of what she could not make out. The girl-boy had clutched the images as if transferring his spirit to them. In the fortress of these squares he could live forever.

She gathered up the pictures on the floor, tore the remaining ones from the girl-boy's hand, and shoved them between her breasts. She understood why the smells had not wilted her. The smell of death was distinctive only when compared to the smell of life. Defeat overtook her like a sickness and she grabbed her belly and vomited. When nothing more would come, her chest still heaved. Her belly ached, her head throbbed, and she barely managed to stagger out of the house.

Getting back home would be almost impossible. The pictures scraped across her breast and stuck to her sweat. She saw Lucinda waiting at her gate as soon she stepped out of Mr. Garvey's house. There she was, hands to her hips, her head cocked to the side to get a better view of the window. The Widow looked around for the rest of the congregation but Lucinda seemed to be alone. *She up to something, that cross-eyed bitch. Them come to kill me for sure.* For a second she thought to go back to Mr. Garvey's house, but the Widow had enough of death for one night, theirs or hers. The more she thought of Lucinda and her stupid ambush, the less she cared. If it was God's will to screw her up again, there was nothing she could do. Except to swing a punch so hard into Lucinda's face that her right eye would become crossed too.

"What you want at me gate, Lucinda?"

She spun around, startled. The Widow stepped closer.

"Oh Heavenly Father! Thank you, Father!"

"Lucinda, me say what you want?"

Lucinda turned away and fidgeted with her skirt.

"Lucinda!"

"Oh God, oh Lord Jesus! The Apostle! Oh Jesus, the Apostle! Oh Jesus Christ Heavenly Father! Him goin kill me, Mary! Him goin kill everybody!"

THE ONE WHO DIP
IS THE ONE WHO KNOW

Them doin nastiness, you know, nasty, nasty nastiness! If God did ever see such nastiness him would a blind!"

"Me look like me care? Come out o me way." The Widow looked around for an ambush.

"Lawd a massy! Me say him goin kill me for running away. Lawd a massy!"

"Really? Somebody want to fix you business? Stand right deh so me can shine light on you!"

"Noooo! Oh Lord. Them goin kill me! Do not leave me out a street."

"Then what me must do, you cross-eye bitch? Help you? No you go bring him here. If chicken come home to roost, don't come hitch up in my coop."

"Lawd, Mary, you a go make them kill me? Is evilness them goin on with. Oh Heavenly Father."

"First you say them doin nastiness, then you say them goin kill you. Is fraid you fraid or is sick you sick? You know what? No bother tell me. Me no business what happen to you."

"What wrong with you? Is why you so cold? Who you think them coming for next, eeh? Look what him do to me."

Mary was surprised that she hadn't seen Lucinda's face before. Her left eye was swollen and her lips wet from blood. Her white dress was torn out of all modesty and her left breast puffed through the ripped cloth. Her feet were bare.

"If me never kick Clarence in him seed, me would a never get away."

This disturbed the Widow in several ways. She and Lucinda had few things in common, one of which was distance, broken only once. Yet here was Lucinda who had forgotten that between them was nothing, not even *Hello*. She had even called her Mary. Seeing Lucinda's bruises was like seeing Lucinda naked. The Widow remembered the feeling of people witnessing her own nakedness. When her husband first saw her out of clothes; her knocked knees, scarred feet, and too-big breasts, which he always attacked first. Lucinda had come into her space as surely as Mr. Greenfield had come. Mary remembered how much she disliked it. Lucinda began to cry.

"Stop the damn bawlin! Stop it, Lucinda!"

Lucinda was a woman accustomed to commands. She stopped.

"Alright, alright, you can come inside."

"Lawd a massy! No! Me step pon fi your lawn, the grass goin kill me for sure!"

"Then what the bloodclaat you think me goin do, carry you?"

"No baba, me nah walk pon that. Look what it do to—"

"Is where him deh? Is where Brother Vix—" The Widow looked around, then glared at Lucinda.

"Don't look pon me, is your house! Oh God! Oh God! Oh God!"

"Shut you damn trap, Lucinda!"

"Them goin kill weeee! Them goin kill weeee!"

"I goin kill you if you don't shut up! We better go inside, all sort of foolishness seem to happen pon this street."

"No sah! Me step pon fi you grass, me dead!"

"Nothing goin happen to you."

"No! Is kill you want to kill me! Just like how them want to kill me! Lord have mercy pon me! What me fi do? What me fi d—"

The Widow slapped the hysterics out of Lucinda's mouth. "Grab me hand. Nothing goin happen to you," she said. Lucinda grabbed without hesitation, squeezing tightly. The Widow dragged her onto the grass. As the blades cut through the spaces between her toes, Lucinda let loose a tiny shriek. They stepped over dead John Crows and spots of blood-darkened grass. The lawn seemed bigger, longer. Maybe it was the tension of Lucinda pulling her back. Lucinda wrung so hard that she pulled her hand loose. The Widow grabbed her quickly, but not before Lucinda screamed. Dew got into the Widow's slippers and made her toes sticky. She blamed Lucinda and hissed. They stepped between a mess of John Crow parts and were finally at the bottom of the steps.

"Lawks! In here so dark!"

"Yes. Night and darkness. One can't happen without the other, but don't tell nobody say me tell you."

"Lawd a massy, ease up pon me, no? You know what me mean. In here daaaaark, boy."

"I don't feel like lighting no candle."

"You don't have no light switch? Me did think this was one of them modern house."

The Widow was glad for statements such as those; Lucinda was always careless with her tongue. Cross-eyed bitch, Mary thought, remembering how much she hated her.

"I don't feel like lighting no candle."

"Alright, alright. Is just that is not my house and me can't see nothing and next thing I goin—"

"Anything in this house belong to you? What you want to see in here?"

"Is just—"

"Is just that you want to poke you head into what goin on in me house. See the door deh, take you backside out!"

"No, Mary! Mary, no! Me can't go out deh so me one! The grass goin kill me!"

"Grass can't kill nobody. Is must—"

"The Devil!"

His name stopped her just as it would anyone in Gibbeah. The Widow had gotten used to not being like everybody else, to not being afflicted with their petty fears. But her enemy's fright infected her.

"You is one damn mad woman. You say the Devil round me house but still you come here. You plan to drive the Apostle out with a pitchfork?"

"I—I—I don't . . . Cho! You confusing me! I . . . Him goin kill me! You no see how him deal with you Pastor? Hector Bligh is here?"

"None of your business."

"Me was just asking. Me know you have to protect you man."

"Him is not me man."

"Him is a man in your house."

"Whatever that mean to you, don't mean so to me."

"Anyway, God know best. Him beat me, you know, Mary. Him beat me. Clarence do it." She pulled down her blouse and her two breasts tumbled out, flapping over the bandages that were wrapped tight around her ribs. The Widow was more disturbed by Lucinda's lack of shame. Her intimacy. This Lucinda whom she did not know well, liked even less, but felt sorry for. The wall between them was eroding, no matter how hard she tried to keep it up. This was a line the Widow could never cross, not even with her husband. She remembered how easy it was, offering him her vagina while holding back herself. Lucinda was making herself open. And honest. That is what disturbed her most about nakedness: the honesty of it.

"Pull down you blouse, Lucinda. Me don't want to see—"

It was too late. There were welts and bruises all over her chest and her neck. Then Lucinda turned her back to the Widow. Bandages hid her skin, but showing through the white were two long streaks of red on the left and right sides of her back. She looked like an angel whose wings had been ripped out. The Widow tasted bile in her mouth and gulped.

"Pull down your blouse, Lucinda."

"Me was the first to want Pastor Bligh gone. Me know. Me sing Hallelujah when the Apostle kick him out. The Bible say forgive seven time upon seven. Me forgive him more than forty-nine time. Me nah lie, me did glad when him get kick out. But Lord, if me did know! Lord, if me did know! Me catch them, you know. That's why Clarence beat me up and me kick him in him seed and run away. Me catch them."

"Catch who?"

"Them. Apostle and Clarence. Me never see nothing lacka that in me life."

"Something evil that you never see? Me did think say God show you everything, like how you and him tight."

"God never show me no man behind man a ram him batty like is girl him a sex."

"What? What you just say?"

"You hear what me say. Clarence and the Apostle naked and him behind the Apostle and him hold on to the Apostle hip, and Clarence ramming the Apostle like him is the husband and the Apostle is the wife."

"You is a lying gal, you know. That is nastiness, even for you."

"How me to lie bout that? No you just say that is *me* did want the Apostle here? Why me would make up something nasty bout him?"

"You up to something. Me know you."

"Me no understand how you no believe me. Like you no see how the two of them tight. Where you think Clarence sleep now?"

"Is lie you a tell. Preacher could a never do them things."

"Like him act like any preacher you know. Me would think that if anybody believe me, it would be you."

"Yeah, and me would believe it if anybody did tell me but you."

"Eh-eh, who you think you is, that me have to prove anything to you? The only reason me come to you is cause you is the only one who eye no blind, not because all of a sudden you so nice and me looking friend."

Lucinda pulled out one of the chairs under the dining table and sat down. She sighed, fingering her mother's ring. The Widow thought to tell her of Mr. Garvey.

"Me never like you, you know, Lucinda. Not even when we was little," she said instead.

"Me know. Me know. Me no take to you neither. But him goin kill me cause me know. And then him goin kill you cause me tell you. And even Pastor Bligh. You no see how the Apostle own the village? Everybody under him control now. Anything him want them to do, them do. Lawd, me no know how things get to this. One day we singing Amazing Grace, next minute we killing old man cause him sexing up cow. Like that is nothing new in country life. Them nearly kill the man who drive the rock-stone truck last week!"

"What you saying to me?"

"You don't know what time clock a strike. Him don't want nobody leaving and nobody coming. Him say sin come in and comtam—constanti—contami— me no remember what him say, but evil might come in the village and we have to keep it out."

"You sound like him still working you."

"No! Him mad! Mad mad mad! And now all o Gibbeah mad too!"

"But people don't just turn crazy so. Me no believe you."

"Eehi, like you no see some of it yourself. You no know people, Mary. Maybe him just giving people what them did always want. That thing in you mind that tickle you, but you would never do."

"And what you always want to do, Lucinda? Me no forget how you did hungry for me man, y'know. Look like you get what you want."

"How anybody could a want that? What you is? A woman or a monster wearing blue dress?"

"Then, then how come you just come to your sense and nobody else?"

"Cause nobody else see what me see in him bedroom. And nobody else goin get kill before anybody find out. He probably call The Five already."

"So you come here cause one of them drop dead when him try cross me lawn. You think that goin save you?"

"No, Pastor Bligh goin save me."

"Listen to you, bout Pastor Bligh. What make you think Pastor Bligh can save anybody?"

"Then him no must! Me no know, but for some reason the Apostle fraid o him like puss. Him don't even want nobody to call the Pastor name."

"Bligh can't even save himself, much less anybody."

For once all hysterics left Lucinda. Her face was grave, with only hiccups betraying the panic that was still in her. "God goin work through him, me know."

The Widow had nothing to say. This was what even she had hoped for, that all his madness should make some bigger sense. Something greater than what she could fathom. But she could never admit this, not to herself and certainly not to Lucinda, whom she now felt compelled to call by her first name.

"You hungry?"

"No."

"You want something to dri—"

"You think him sleeping?"

"I . . . Wait here."

She had spent too much time outside his door. The Widow had fed him pens, pencils, chalk, and charcoal. Would he have pricked himself and written in blood? The Widow would rather not answer. He was mad as raas. And yet she knew Jesus was working through him. He had to be. This madness must make bigger sense. Everything that was not of the Lord fell dead at her gate. That had to be him—Bligh, not the Lord. He had drawn a line in the spirit around her house. It did not make her feel safe or protected, only secure in the knowledge of death. The Widow raised her hand to knock, but he had already opened the door.

She had fooled herself; of course her heart could sink lower. The room stank with the air of the old. She thought that if Mr. Greenfield had died here, this is what the room would have smelt like. The little she saw of the writing she could not understand. A frenzied scrawl of words and marks, some running into each other. He had written on his chest as well, a parade of symbols that made no sense. Bligh scratched his nose and she saw his fingers, the tips blackened with ink and coal. His hair seemed to be whiter. He was shirtless.

"Lucinda . . . she . . ."

He looked right, left, then straight at her.

"Lucinda . . . she want you. She saying some things bout the Apostle. She—"

He stepped back and closed the door. The Widow was unsure what to feel. Better to give up on all feeling and have a good night's sleep. Better peace than understanding. Tonight anyway. *Him can turn a mad raas, for all I care.* But she was wearing blue because of him. She could admit this now. No, her own mind countered, better to turn away. Better to have peace, because peace was nothing. Nothing was the only thing you could cut by half and still have too much. But as she turned away, he opened the door again. He was fully dressed in his white suit, which was covered with words, scrawls, and shapes. He seemed older, but also taller; the words reached upwards, climbing toward his head. Standing straight and firm, he said things without speaking.

"Oh bless God! Oh praise Jesus! Oh praise the Lord!" said Lucinda.

Bligh stood still, staring at Lucinda as seconds grew pregnant and both women grew tense. Lucinda looked away and began to fidget. The Widow found the broom in the corner of the room. She feigned to sweep but released it to fall back into the corner. Lucinda sat down again, her fingers mid-fidget.

"So," the Widow and the sister said at once.

"So what you goin do?" Lucinda blurted out quickly. "You hear what him doin? Nastiness, I tell you is pure nast—"

"You see him doing nastiness?" His stare could cut through iniquity like a thin blade of judgment and get to truth. Too much for Lucinda, who preferred truth that pointed no finger at her.

"Ah . . . well, sexing. Me see them sexing!"

"How?"

"What?" the Widow said.

"What you mean?" said Lucinda.

"How. How were they sexing?"

"Like how man and woman sexing. Nasty nastiness."

"Tell me."

"Really, Hector, nobody have to tell anybody—" started the Widow.

"The Apostle bend over pon the vanity and Clarence behind him a ram him like man dog."

"You're lying," said Pastor Bligh.

"No! Look how Clarence beat me. Them is sodomite!"

"True. But you didn't see it."

"Me hear it."

"No. You didn't hear it either."

"Well, Clarence over him house night and day. What that suppose to mean?" She looked at him, hungry for an answer. "So, so what you goin do? You goin kill him?"

"You mad?" the Widow shouted. She had expected the Pastor's rebuke to be stronger. That he would kick her blinkin backside out of the house with the boot of the Holy Spirit. But he said nothing, and neither did Lucinda. Her outburst was left hanging, staining the quiet like an unwanted intrusion.

"Eeh? Eeh, Pastor? You no see say the Devil come to steal, kill, and destroy? Him rob you job and kill Massa Fergie and him doing nastiness with man. Oh Lord Jesus, what him goin do when him find out say me is here?"

"Thou shalt not kill," the Widow said feebly as she turned to walk away. But then she remembered that this was her house and nobody was going to make her feel uncomfortable. She sat at the dining table eyeing Lucinda hard.

"So you goin—"

"Enough." He turned his back to them and stooped down. Sometimes he would close his eyes and whisper. The Widow thought it was a prayer for things he had forgotten to say before. He did this until morning came.

Lucinda woke up first. She looked down and saw Pastor Bligh fully prostrate, his white suit covered in marks that she recognized from the Apostle's books. The Widow slept in the chair, her chin resting on her chest as she snored.

Lucinda stepped over the Pastor and tiptoed down the hallway. She passed the kitchen and a closed bedroom, afraid that she would wake up the Widow but excited by the same. She continued down the hall, stopping at the only room with the door open. She knew this was where the Pastor slept. Or whatever he did at night. But the Pastor had stopped sleeping. There was God's work to do. Her surprise quickly gave way to a curiosity as deep as her lusts.

The words scribbled on the walls stirred her. Some she could recognize; names such as Daniel, James, and John. There were words that she could not pronounce. They seemed to dance and swirl from floor to ceiling, even the ones that were jagged and mad. There were numbers as well. Sixes and sevens and groups and signs. Triangles and eyes. A goat's head. Stars and crosses and the smudge of ideas aborted and erased. The words broke distinction between floor and wall, wall and ceiling. At any minute they would leap from their surfaces and attack her. They would swirl and twirl and wrap themselves around her neck.

She turned around and he was there. At that second she remembered her nose swimming in the hair of another man's chest and the whip slashing her back to set her straight.

"It's time," Bligh said. The Widow was still asleep.

"Everybody stop work, you know. Him tell everybody who go out o village to stop work. Him say everything we want, God will provide. All we need to do is stretch it. Everybody chicken must now go in one coop."

He motioned her to be silent. She was accustomed to commands.

"A preacher must never forget the mistake he makes as a man, or he's goin to start think he is God. You understand, woman?"

"Y-yes."

"No you do not. God chose not to reveal it you. Only He knows why. And what must happen, must happen. What day is today?"

"Thursday."

"Thursday."

"Him sleep til 9 o'clock most mornin. What you goin do, kill him? Plead the blood of Jesus? Is demon him have? Me see it one time, you know. Me see the demon attack him in the office and him run me out cause him head take him. You goin drive out the demons? No that you did try when you and him catch up in church? Him did tell me to tell people say you kill him and him come back to life."

"So why do it when you know better?"

"I . . . I don't know. I just did want one man . . . just one man, one time to . . . You goin try drive out the evil spirit again?"

"Lucas York doesn't have any demon, woman," he said, closing the door behind her. "He has syphilis."

The clock above the dining table struck half past 6. Outside, the trees, grass, and dirt were all a deep morning yellow. The road was silent, exhausted from all-night service. Hector did not move with joy. That was gone; all that was left was purpose. As he passed the Widow, his hand grazed her shoulder and his purpose was forgotten. She was still asleep. He knelt down in front of her as Lucinda fidgeted. Her snore had petered out to the heavy inhale and exhale of an inflamed sinus. He touched her face and her breathing fell quiet. The house was still save for the shuffle of Lucinda's feet. He looked at the Widow as if he saw her for the first time. Sleep softened wrinkles that had come to her face too early. Hector brushed away hair that had stuck to the sweat on her forehead and moved to touch her lips, but stopped. He took her left hand that had fallen away and placed it in her lap. She shifted slightly, but he was already out the door.

"Lawd a massy, wait no, you walk too fast!"

"Too fast for who?"

"Too fast fi me poor corn toe. You think you can heal me too?"

He did not answer.

Outside, the sky was clear. The Widow's house was at the corner of Brillo and Hanover roads. The church was at the foot of Hanover Road, not much of a journey. Yet he had barely gone ten paces when he saw Mrs. Fracas across the road as if she never left or came. A couple yards down was Mrs. Smith-field, and nearer to him, close enough to hear his breathing, was Brother Jakes. The Pastor wondered if he was blind, for he had not seen anyone be-fore. Along the strip of road they stood and more were coming. Men, women, and children. Fear was not of the Lord, but terror vanquished him. In his mind went off a million panics. Two more of The Five were on the other side of the road, but they began walking as he passed them, their gait matching his. They stopped when he stopped and strode when he strode.

"Lucinda, you . . ." He turned around. She had not gone further than the Widow's gate. Behind him were three of The Five, which now included Clarence, who had replaced Brother Vixton. The other two crossed the road, coming toward him. The Rum Preacher ran, but his flight was fruitless. Clarence struck him with a rock and he fell. They kicked, stomped, punched, and subdued him. The village looked on, but stayed in place as the screams of the Pastor echoed from fence to fence. Having punched two teeth loose, Brother Jakes was satisfied. The others stepped away as he grabbed the Pastor by one foot and dragged him all the way up to the church.

MAKING PLANS FOR THURSDAY

*L*ucinda had been to the Majestic Cinema only once, when she was twelve. This secret she shared with a dead road, away from the busy street, that took her there and back hidden in a thatch of lusty green leaves. Lucinda arrived late and hid at the back of the cinema so that nobody could see her. Because of this she never knew what the name of the film was, but she remembered the man—a white man with slicked black hair, a mustache, and big ears—as he grabbed the woman who seemed to resist and comply, and carried her up a flight of steps so high they seemed to lead to Heaven. She knew what they went upstairs to do. Country girls had little time for sentimentality, that was the province of white women. She knew that the stairway led to what her mother did for seven shillings and a pence, but even her mother wanted, even once, for a man to carry her. It angered Lucinda that her mother might have shared the same want and the same loss. But she was not her mother, she told herself for the thousandth time. Apostle York was hers. He would grab her by the waist and tell her an embarrassing childhood secret, and it would be strange and funny, and she would laugh her little girl's laugh, and he would kiss her the way men kiss women, and fuck her, and say words like *fuck* in a breathy whisper, for she was his Mary and his whore. And he would be her calm and her storm, and in this new wind, she and the Apostle would be gone. Soon.

Soon was today. The day she turned the Rum Preacher over to The Five and still had time to make the Apostle a special breakfast. Even through a swollen eye she could see there was promise to the morning. The kitchen was part of the church, separate from the Apostle's quarters. She began cooking, forgetting dumplings for johnnycakes, calalloo for bacon, ackee for eggs—

whatever smart people, good-blooded people, white people, ate. At the bottom of the pot she saw her reflection and winced. Clarence had beaten her with no regret. The Apostle had the idea. He needed to weed out the evil that lived in the Widow's house and reach the lost at any cost.

"We must save the lost, Lucinda," the Apostle had said to her an hour before she took her battered self to the Widow. "We must save the lost, but first we must stop the man who lost them. Are you ready to save the lost at any cost, Lucinda?"

"Yes, Apostle."

"Good. You're my hound, Lucinda, and he's a jinnal, just like a fox. When a fox is hiding in his hole there's only one thing we can do."

"Flood the hole, Apostle?"

"Flood the? What? No, no, my simple child, when a fox runs to his hole you have to flush the bastard out. You have to flush him out."

"How we flush him, Apostle?"

"Not we, *you*. He has to believe you, Lucinda. Thank the Lord that He has chosen you for this serious, serious task. You are first among women! Thank the Lord that He has predestined you to go into the enemy's camp. All we have to do know is make him believe you. That old bastard can read faces, Lucinda, we have to make sure that he reads only one thing."

Then he set Clarence upon her like a dog. She could see his enjoyment; the glimmer of comeuppance in his eye. This was his revenge for the whipping. But the Son had to suffer before he was glorified. So did Job. And Jacob. And Jeremiah and Paul. This was God's work and He would reward her with love. The Apostle's love, which would be a reflection of God. York would be her sun and she would be his moon, reflecting his light and blinding those underneath her. But Clarence wore the Apostle's clothes now. She dismissed such things with logic. After all, *how would a empty-pocket bad-breed nayga like Clarence afford good clothes, now that him get promoted?* She knew who had the Apostle's heart. That was why he asked her to make the sacrifice, to go into the Preacher's camp and lure him out. This was no different from the father asking the son, so that afterward the son would sit at the right hand of the father.

She smiled at having served the Apostle so well. Memory had deceived her before, but this morning Lucinda indulged the past as she broke three eggs in corn oil and sprinkled them with salt and pepper. *Nasty nayga bitch, I can smell you fishy from here,* a voice said. *You think any man would a want you now that you pokie dry up?*

Her mother came with the smell of vinegar. Country legend had it that if somebody's blood was on your hands, their ghost lived with you forever.

"Dry-up pokie never stop *you* from taking man," Lucinda replied.

You think you good. Only me know say you wicked. Just like you father who don't stay.

"Is you why him leave."

You pokie stink. Only evil go in a it and only evil come out of it. The river tell me bout you.

"Yes, yes, me born evil. Me born bad. No your pokie me come out of?"

Bad seed. Bad from the day you born when me try fi kill you. But the birth cord never wrap round you neck tight enough.

"Eehi, and look how cock mouth catch cock. You should a try harder. What you do to me, me come back and do to you. Only me finish the job."

Lucinda.

"Don't *Lucinda* me. My man goin stay with me, you watch. Him not goin run way. Him not goin hate me so much that him sleep with goat instead. Now get out of me kitchen. Nasty nayga bitch."

Lucinda broke into "Old Rugged Cross," just in case any other spirit decided to attack her thoughts this morning. The Apostle said nothing should stand in the way of her joy. "Old Rugged Cross"! Two johnnycakes and three strips more of bacon and breakfast would be ready.

She flipped a johnnycake and felt sorry for the Widow. Lucinda was surprised at her own tenderness. Perhaps now that she had won, she could feel compassion. The sympathy the victorious felt for the defeated, the slayer felt for the dead, the Roman for the crucified Christ. The Widow now had nothing. Lucinda had promise. Promise was a pink ray in the morning sky and a silent twinkle on unopened flowers. Promise was the sun peeking through louver windows and kissing her on the cheek. Maybe the Widow would find Christ again. Now that the Rum Preacher was driven from her house, perhaps the Widow would find peace. She would reach out in friendship, though they could never be friends, of course. Lucinda remembered how envy made a monster out of herself; how much worse would it do to a woman who cursed God and lost her man twice?

On the way to Apostle's house, she almost skipped, but stopped when the orange juice glasses shook. She giggled at the smell of eggs, bacon, and toast, her white man's breakfast. She would wake the Apostle and call him by his first name. She paused. Lucinda had no idea what his first name was. No matter, this would be a morning of new discoveries. She would wake him up and serve breakfast in bed, and who knows, climb in under sheets that smelt of his sweat and feed him. She knew from cleaning once a week that the doors were always unlocked.

"What you was doing, laying the damn eggs yourself?"

Clarence pulled his pants up and flicked his penis through the fly. Lucinda froze as her own mind attacked her, molested her with information she did not want and could not process. She was a simple woman who concluded simply. *Clarence naked. Clarence pulling up him pants. Clarence cocky dangling like a sausage outside him pants. Clarence pulling up him pants but don't have no brief underneath. Clarence in the Apostle bedroom naked. Clarence pulling up him pants. Clarence cocky dangling like sausage outside him pants. Clarence in the Apostle room and him . . . him . . . him picking up him shirt off the floor.*

"Well, what you waiting for, blessed assurance? Put down the tray and get out."

She was a simple woman who concluded simply. She placed the tray on the bed and stood up straight and stiff. Lucinda could not look at him, nor could she bear the sound of the toilet flushing, the inevitable emergence of *him*, the proof of nothing. Inside her was nothing. She heard her mother chuckle.

"Bitch, at least close the door when you leaving."

Lucinda ran back to the church. She ran past the kitchen and the mess of egg shells, raw bacon, spilt flour, and squeezed oranges on the counter. She ran all the way upstairs to her room and shut the door. They were waiting for her. In the mirror she saw them: her mother and Night Lucinda, at times two, at times one, all the time laughing like the crackle of lightning.

GOLGOTHA, OR THE INCIDENT

A bba babba a maka desh.

We pray to the living God who is the Father and the Son through the Vicar of God who sits pon the left hand of the Father. The Vicar is the creation of the Son who is one with the Son but also the Father.

Rekelo baba lacosa.

We have come to bring praise to he who is most high. We enter his gates with thanksgiving and his courts with praise. We present ourselves as the living sacrifice entreating the Father to receive the Son of the Son in his most Holy place.

Sikosa rabokok mieshande ribobaba.

The enemy we defeat. Is so prophecy go. The walker in darkness get bring into the light. We thank the Mighty One for victory over the kingdom of spirits. We thank the Father and send the servant of darkness back into darkness.

Oh bababa lajakmeh sikethacoco.

Amen.

The Widow woke up to a threat. One more minute and the pictures would have cut through skin. She reached for them between dress and breast. The Widow placed them on the table like cards and studied them carefully. They were all faded to sepia and they all provoked the same response. Boys, some small and featureless, some with more than a few facial and pubic hairs, all in undress. Some had their legs crossed, some were spread wide like cherubs caught in knowledge of their sex. They were no longer boys but dolls, warped and reshaped into somebody's reflection. Like the girls on those playing cards that Mr. Greenfield kept in his secret place. In all her years of suspecting Mr. Garvey of sodomy and seeing his several nephews, she never married the two. Her mind traveled to places she had not thought thinkable. Such sickness and perversion tormented her, reduced her to a child's fear of darkness. She looked at pictures of boys, spread like women, some in makeup and hats, and she imagined demons raping tiny holes of innocence and inexperience. There were others that needed no imagining, their buttocks free but their mouths stuffed with what went beyond her ability to believe. The only way to pull herself out was to imagine them unreal, or French, as her husband would have said to explain anything obscene. That was the only way she knew to make them unremarkable, to take her heart out. She would have succeeded were it not for the third photograph, which she had passed over twice. The picture had blurred into the others before, but now a face slid into focus.

From a mop of wild black hair, the signs came. Eyes sparkled from brown skin that was light but darker than the others. The same brown skin, the same eyes, and the same wet, unruly hair that blew over his shoulders even in the stillness of the picture.

"Hector! Hector! Hector! Come quick! Hect—" A silence came upon her, overwhelmed her completely. The quiet punished her for perception. The Widow remained standing, accepting his absence from the house. Her blue dress seemed a stupid thing. She no longer wished to wear it. She wanted to peel the memory of him, the musk of him, away from her skin. The stench of dead John Crows drifted through the house. She went into his room and sat amid a confluence of words and symbols. She remained there until nightfall.

Abba babba a maka desh.

We declare the Kingdom of 1000 years. To the light of the Father and soon-coming King. We His other sheep bow down before Him. We invoke His presence in the name of the Most High.

Friday morning broke through the gray sky. The Rude Boys were already up. They had a big job and big tools to match. The noise they made had the rhythm of industry, the clang, crunch, and smash of purpose. Hammers and pickax clubbed away, setting off shards that ricocheted off the bridge. The Apostle gave them until 1:30.

"You know, they used to keep uppity niggers in line with that thing round your neck. What d'you make of that?" said the Apostle as he saw the Pastor. The room was dusky and Bligh's neck was in shackles, which The Five found in Brother Vixton's house. A chain went from the ceiling to Bligh's neck, holding him in place. His hands were tied behind him. "I'm figuring you had some schooling, so I know that you see the irony in this, this being your room."

"The syphilis rot out your mind."

"Now there's a thought. But what do I know about thinking, I have syphilis. How did you know, by the way?"

"You see plenty when you preach in hospital. Lucas."

The Apostle froze. "A hospital in Kingston? I see."

"Yes, Kingston. Lucas."

"Lucas York is dead. I killed him myself."

"You're not dead. Just sick."

"Sick? That's all? Three months of sparring and all you can call me is sick? Come now, Bligh, only that? That Sunday you knew me more than any man or woman, or God for that matter, and you still don't know the half. You know I'm not possessed, that was your mistake, and yet spirits are all around me. I can get one to fuck you if you wish. Think of it as a goodbye gift."

"Keep your damn demon," Bligh said, looking at his feet.

"Just between you and me, I think they prefer spirits. Well, if you don't want that kind of spirit, how about the other kind? Can't you feel it? That whiskey calling you like a girl who never says no?"

"No."

"Nobody would blame you, Bligh, if you disappeared in a whiskey bottle right now. It might even save you. Should I get some? How about Johnny Walker Red, though you strike me more as a Black? You know, I had this hunch you'd say yes, so look what I brought."

In the Apostle's hand was a bottle of whiskey, glimmering with gold.

"Keep your liquor. I have the Holy Spirit."

"And how is that going for you? Are you quenched? Are you in high spirits? Or would you prefer this one? I can keep a secret."

"I don't want it—"

"You don't want it straight or you don't want it now?"

"I don't want it ever."

"Ever. That's a mighty long time. Maybe you've just forgotten the taste, now that you're so righteous and all. Poor little whiskey, dying from jealousy. 'If only he could taste me,' she said. If only." The Apostle pulled the cap and held the bottle over Bligh's head. "'If only he could taste me,' she said." He poured the whiskey over Bligh's forehead. Hector shut his eyes tight as Johnny Walker ran down his face and wetted his lips.

"Just stick that big tongue out, there's a good lad," said the Apostle. "One sip, Bligh. Come now, Bligh, the whiskey's a-wasting. Bligh? Bliiiiiigh. Look at that now, all done. No more whiskey. You try to give black people things and—"

"God curse you."

"I think you got the tense wrong. But that's fine, God curse me? I curse him back." Apostle York sat down in the room's one chair which leaned against the doorway.

"The Bible is just a book, Bligh. An incomplete, inconclusive book. Your church calls itself the Church of St. Thomas, and yet your same church forbids the Gospel of St. Thomas. There's so much, Bligh, so much your ignorant little negro mind can't comprehend. Like Solomon. I've read books of Solomon that you've never heard of."

"This is history class or you just love talk?"

"No, this isn't history, this is the present. But you'll soon be—history, that is."

"Black arts goin kill you."

"Black arts? Black arts? You mean magic? This isn't magic, fool. This is the true work of God!"

"It will kill you."

"It keeping me alive! No doctor could help me. By the time they found out what I was suffering from, I was as good as fucked. But I don't need no physician, I am the great physician. God. You see God? God is a figment. A level. A process. I followed the same process and I became God."

"Now I know you mad. Nobody can become God. God was never born and will never die, He is the I am."

"Lie. Darkness made Him, light shape Him, and people colored up the ugly parts. You, Bligh, you same one; if you close your eyes right now and pray to God, you think of somebody who looks exactly like me. My hair, my beard, my eyes, my skin—"

"Your pox."

"To Hell with you."

"Is not me Satan waiting on."

"How you figure that?"

"You go and sin with your privates and catch a disease and now you blame God. How long since you get it?"

"Get it? You talk as if I had it coming. This was given to me, Bligh. Call it God's gift. God gave syphilis to me."

"Blasphemy. God don't give disease, He is the healer. You telling a lie."

"I am the way and the truth."

"The father of lies."

"Gibbeah would rather have my lies than your truth. Why do they follow me so easily, Bligh? So quick, without question? I give them something God can't give. Listen, I'm taking this whole village down with me. You should have left when you had the chance. You don't belong here."

"Neither do you. These people didn't do you nothing—"

"You fucking idiot! How far, eh? How far must a knife go in your chest before you realize you're being fucked with? How do you think I know every name? How do you think I recognize every face? I was here, Hector. I was here even when Uncle Aloysius brought your sorry, drunk arse to Gibbeah. The only reason that man hired you is because you were as blind then as you are now. Not so mad now, eh? This syphilis came from God. From the man of God who preceded you. Aloysius Garvey's good friend and rape-mate. Is it coming to you now? Why don't you say his name with me? Yes, Pastor

Palmer. I have the scars to prove it, shall I drop my pants and show you?"

"No."

"Look at that, a Pastor who couldn't keep his cock in his pants. Sound like anybody you know?"

"God was with you. Even then, God was with you."

"No. God was with the preacher who was lying in the bed with me. But you know, I'm starting to feel redeemed. Thank you, Bligh, thank you. I think I'm believing this Bible now; that God suffers with me, really, I do. I can just see Him crucified by his own father for kicks. God didn't help me. He could have given me freedom, but He didn't. He could have given me joy or peace, but He didn't. You didn't even notice me. Not even once. I leave a year after you came and you didn't even notice."

The Apostle coughed, blinking his eyes until the wet glimmer of tears was gone.

"But I don't blame you. I blame God. At the very least, He could have made me not feel the fucking pain, but He didn't. God left me and forsook me, so I did the same to that son of a bitch. You know what I did? I studied him. I read everything from Apocrypha to Luther to Augustine to Faust. And I read more. And I learned something. God is real, Jehovah is a myth. Jehovah is a thing people invent to excuse horrible shit as if it had some purpose. But there is none, you see, that's what Satan knew all along. There is no purpose. There's no meaning, no teaching, no greater good to come out of sucking my fake uncle's cock. There's just my mouth and his cock. Nothing else. Like God, God is nothing. I used God's nothing to become something, and damn if I'm not dragging God to Hell with me."

"No."

"Then I started to read people who realized what I did, that God had a limit. Stuff from Solomon. That lying Bible would tell you that Solomon got stupid when he strayed; no, he got even more wise. That's when he started making sense. He could command angels and demons and gain wisdom that God had been fearing from man ever since Eve bit the apple. Knowledge, Bligh. That's how you become God. Now angels and demons do my will too."

"No."

"Then I came back. You think Uncle was happy to see me? Him and his new batch of boys? You know what he did when we got too strong for him?

Send us off to boarding school for more men to fuck with us. But I came back. I came back in the same clothes his preacher friend used to wear. The skinny black fucker thought I came bringing forgiveness, until he saw my sword. Cutlass, actually. Chop his head clean off. Then I chopped off his curse. Then I chopped up every little new demon he was growing in that house. Most of them were still sleeping when I send them to Hell."

"No."

"No? Not at all. I belong here, Bligh. I belong with these people. I belong with all these fuckers who suspected or even knew what my uncle was, but let their nigger ways allow it. And those same nigger ways now allowing me.

"I belong here. I drove you out but you wouldn't leave. Now I can't do anything for you."

12:15. Apostle York had said 2:00. He declared it last night. Mrs. Fracas was getting ready. She had not worn the black dress since Lillamae's funeral. She cursed it for being the most expensive yet least useful dress. But the Lord had taught her that what seems useless may have not yet come into purpose. People were like that too. She looked at herself in the mirror and saw the miraculous slimming powers of pin stripe. God was going to use her as his instrument today.

Deacon Pinckney used his two good eyes to admire himself in his mirror. Tony Curtis had no black so he wore white: his grandfather's pants and his mother's blouse.

Clarence's tie was crooked. From behind and facing the mirror, the Apostle tugged until it was straight. He smoothed out the shoulders of his jacket, then handed him pants to match.

Brother Jakes picked out a black veil for his wife, who had before decided not to go. The swelling around her battered eye signified her change of heart. A long dress made sure that her whipped thighs and bruised hands would be concealed as well. Even the children were dressed and ready.

The Rude Boys were finished. Two o'clock came and passed, so they left the tools and went home to change. The bridge had fallen to a cataclysmic crash, the sound of life coming undone, collapsing and killing other lives underneath. Through a series of night services the Apostle had shown them how it was possible. God's people only needed God after all. York was serious.

The children were restless. Most were upset enough about wearing Sunday clothes on a Sunday, but this was Friday. Some of the children wondered why they stopped going to the school ten miles down past the valley. Today they were bound in stiff pants and starched shirts and dresses and shoes sent in barrels from *Englan* and *New Yawk* along with wide ties made for adults. The Pastor had told them that they were going to play a new game. And God wanted them looking their best.

Brother Jakes's oldest son had also decided not to come. His subsequent brutal beating sealed his own prophecy. This was not a day for children to disobey fathers; this was a day to submit to Apostle York as if to God. This was the day that the Lord had made, and this was His work. Clarence dressed the Apostle. He straightened his necktie and wiped away lines of dirt from York's shoes with his fingers. Clarence then guided the robes over the Apostle's head gently, so that his hands slipped through the sleeves. The layers of cloth fell around him like a shower. Clarence gave the Apostle his red book and his black book, then he gave him something else.

The front door swung open and the Widow leapt through yelling.
"Is what unu do with him? Is what unu do wi—" The street was empty. The silence stunned her. Usually, if given time, the street could answer any question. But Brillo Road refused her. The Widow felt alone, more alone than she did in her empty house.

Mary.

She turned around, but no one was there. She went back inside the house. It was different now, smelling of neither her, Mr. Greenfield, nor the Pastor.

A new smell that was already an old one; a familiar one whose meaning she knew. She knew the voice as well. The Widow went to the kitchen and took out the chicken that she had already seasoned. She turned on the gas stove. Then she went into the bedroom and took out another blue dress.

Lucinda was in her room combing her hair in two and plaiting the ends. She had heard the Apostle's decree and though told to stay away, she put on her mother's black dress anyway. It was only fitting, she had become her mother, another woman for whom men reflected the failure of life. She heard whispers coming from the mirror. Outside, below her, the dust awoke.

The Apostle stood at the door of the church looking out. He licked his lips and tasted the person behind him. "Clarence, tell the people that God is ready."

Sikasa raboka makasetha likoso.

Go down Emmanuel Road
Gal an boy
Fi go broke rock-stone
Go down Emmanuel Road
Gal an boy
Fi go broke rock-stone
Broke them one by one
Gal an boy
Broke them two by two
Gal an boy

Finger mash don't cry
Gal an boy
Remember a play we deh play

Since the truck stop come and gone, plenty rock-stone did leave. The Apostle say the truck bring evil spirit back into the village and anything of evil we have to cut it out! Cut it out! Cut it out!

A few came before, a few after, but most came at once, gathering in a jagged circle near the bridge where the stonebreakers used to work. The wind stirred up marl dust and grayed black jackets, dresses, and pants. Mrs. Fracas brought her umbrella. The only thing Estrella had that was black was her miniskirt. Nobody noticed. Brother Jakes stood up with more than enough pride for his ashamed wife and missing son. Mrs. Smithfield waved her hands to fan her face against the heat. A mumble rose but fell as soon as they saw the Apostle coming behind Clarence, who cradled his red and black books. He waved his fingers and the choir, scattered among the crowd, began to sing "Amazing Grace."

"I say this unto you. Listen to what the Lord is saying, you followers of John Eight, verse seven. You hear the scriptures incorrectly. You misinterpret the word of the Father and as such are deceived by the Devil. When the Lord asked for he who is without sin to cast the first stone, He spoke to Jews and to Gentiles. We are neither Jew nor Gentile but Christian. To those who are reborn of the Lord we are no longer with sin. And if you are in Him you are a new . . ."

"Creation."

"I said, if you are in him you are a new . . ."

"NEW CREATION!"

"Hallelujah! Praise God!" He waved his hand and suddenly there was a scuffle and a shout. From behind the church they came. Three of The Five, dressed in black and dragging the Rum Preacher. Bligh tripped. Deacon Pinckney picked up the chain and pulled him through the dirt. The Preacher held onto the chain lest the deacon break his neck. The other three flanked but did not touch him as he rolled and scraped against the gravel and marl. The Preacher mumbled to himself. The children thought he was a mad animal.

The deacon was enjoying this too much. He yanked with force where none was necessary, sometimes facing the crowd and smiling as he did so. Each time the Preacher tried to walk, the deacon would pull, and Bligh would fall, the ground bruising his skin. The white marl made him ghostly. He was a wraith; a trapped night spirit brought out into day. His eyes were red, the only sign that within him ran blood. Deacon Pinckney pulled until he was in the center of the circle. The children gawked, the men and women thought of punishment and stayed fixed on the Apostle.

"Father, we obey Your decree of First Corinthians. Today we expel the man who was once our brother, but is now a vessel of iniquity. And so, Father, we send him back from whence he came. Back to Hell with his father, Satan. Gibbeah makes an atonement in bloo—"

"You . . . y . . . can't . . . even . . . say . . ."

"Oh! Abba babba a maka desh! Oh libreh cassakokah maka desh! Oh consuming fire, lion of the tribe of Judah! Abba Father! Rebethababa Lakosa!"

"Father, forgive him . . ."

"Back! Back! I bind you in the name of the Morning Star! I bind you! I bind you, Hector Blight! You are a blight on God's precious fabric, a—"

"Gibbe . . . him can't . . . say . . . na—"

"A stain on the curtain of Heaven!"

"Jesu . . ."

Deacon Pinckney struck him with his foot. The Preacher bit his tongue and spat blood.

"No! Don't look into the eyes of evil! He prowls like a roaring lion looking for souls to devour. Done with the man of darkness. We shall obey the star of the morning!"

"The star of the morning is Lucif—"

"Today is the final victory. Even now God is building His wall and enclosing His Kingdom. Just like Masada! Ayeh babacosa maka desh! From this day forth, Gibbeah shall always be in His presence. Suffer the children first!"

The children knew what to do. They ran quickly, returning when their hands were full. The Apostle raised both hands and Clarence raised both books.

"The scripture—"

"You never touch . . . scripture in y . . . life . . . Solomon fall . . . your fall . . ."

"Enough with the Devil talk!" The adults picked up rocks and flung. The children flung as if for sport. Deacon Pinckney flung with the force of a cricketer. The women held nothing back. Those whose hands were empty ran for more. The Preacher had prayed for strength, but he screamed.

"I see . . . Heaven open," Bligh said, "I see Heav . . ."

Rocks punched their way through his flesh. A rain of rocks crushed his face and tore off his jaw. Rocks broke his hand and punctured his back and broke his skull open for pink to run through. Bligh spat his lifeblood out and it spread across the ground like the shadow of wings.

In mere minutes his body was broken and he was dead. The crowd continued until he was almost entombed in rock. The Apostle raised two fingers and they stopped.

"Behold, He cometh with clouds! And every eye shall see Him and they also who pierced Him, and all the kindreds of the Earth shall wail because of Him. Even so, Amen!

"I am the Alpha and the Ome—"

The Apostle was interrupted by the slightest of touches. A splash of white hit his shoulder and flowed down his sleeve. He looked over at the nearly covered body of the Pastor Bligh. A bird had landed on top of the stones. A dirty white bird, a dove. It hopped from stone to stone carelessly.

"I am the Alpha and the Omega! The beg—"

"RAASCLAAT!"

Mrs. Fracas pointed above and there they were. A cloud of doves in a shifty circle of white that eclipsed the sun. The children ran first but too late. In one swoop they dove into the crowd, screeching and ripping hair and flesh with claws and beaks. Brother Jakes, as he pulled two from his chest, left his face unprotected. The last thing he would see were clawed feet coming toward his eyes and the red spurt of his own blood. The birds fluttered and flapped and screamed along with the people's screams. Mrs. Fracas, her hair knotted in birds, swung her umbrella and struck her own child. The stampede of adults trampled the children not swift enough to run out of the way. And yet more doves came, digging holes in Clarence's face and tearing wordless pages from the Apostle's books. They picked and clawed at Mrs. Smithfield's daughter's feet and she screamed. As she bent to grab those at her feet a dove landed square in her face, slashing her nose and cheek. Birds killed themselves by crashing into walls and fences, and pushed one of The Five over the edge where the bridge used to be. Deacon Pinckney stumbled and landed head first, snapping his neck. In the grocery there was an explosion followed by the *whoomph!* of a fire. The doves flew all the way down Brillo Road, chasing the village and ripping the skin of those who fell. They flew through doors that failed to close in time and chased children into small closets. Lucinda, watching the dust below, did not see the horde of birds before they burst through her window, shattering the glass. She screamed and swung, but they dug into her flesh with tiny, sharp beaks that tore her clothes. A dove hopped on her back and scratched through her cuts. She ran around the room as the dove's wings flapped from her back. Outside, they knocked over stands and carts and flew into glass windows breaking their necks.

Then the doves flew away.

In the center where the stoning took place, rocks were scattered in every direction, but the Pastor's body was gone. People shuddered in their homes. They had not seen the bridge fall, but reeled under the weight of loneliness.

The Apostle had no bruise or scrape. Nobody had seen him flee. He was in front of the Widow Greenfield's house as the sun began to fall. He stood for several minutes before making the first step. Though his legs rose and fell with movement, his feet never touched the ground until his shoe tapped the Widow's doorstep.

The door was open. The smell of burnt meat flew at him. Her table was set for two and from the bathroom came the steady patter of the shower. In the bedroom was her dress, pressed and laid out on the bed. The Widow was gone. The Apostle smiled to himself and left, but as he passed the table, what he saw crippled his spirit. A photograph, faded to sepia but still appalling in its detail. A boy of eleven, unwise to the world, yet deep in the knowledge of his sex. A boy who posed like a girl and received Aloysius Garvey and his fat preacher friend like a whore. A brown boy with wet, unruly black hair that glimmered like a thousand tiny eyes. The Apostle was racked with shudders. He could neither cry nor scream. *Lucas*, said a voice. The Apostle's lips formed the shape of the word "Uncle," but this he could not say. Hopelessness overcame him, but rage as well. He slammed his fist on the table, breaking it in two. Outside, the sky gathered clouds through which the dying sun shot the redness of October. Rain would fall soon.

RECKONING

Sunlight twisted and danced through leaves to hit the ground in bold yellow strokes. The trees were greener than anyone had ever seen them. There was no movement, only light. Three rainy months had passed since Gibbeah burnt their fallen brothers, sisters, sons, and daughters, and life was a blessing. This was the prophecy. God had not left nor forsaken them, for they had food and they had fellowship.

One month after the village killed Hector Bligh, Lucinda was buried in the church cemetery. She had leapt from her room window, prompted by three voices that spoke to her in the shattered mirror. Lucinda had flung herself to the ground on a Saturday afternoon and on her back was a dead dove, its wings spread wide.

Nobody approached the Widow's house. The Apostle decreed that it should be left alone; a reminder of the consequence of disobedience, the greatest sin. Gibbeah would be the most holy place. An Old Testament place. Soon the Lord would return and He would make His dwelling here, for they had the fragrance of worthiness. And why should the Lord not make His home in Gibbeah? He once made His home in Bethlehem, a ghetto then as now. Galilee, where even the people stunk of fish. And Capernaum, which was worse than Galilee. No, the Lord was coming. The sky would fall and down would come chariots of light carrying the Heavenly host.

Children were most useful to the Kingdom. The Apostle taught school himself. The School of Boy Prophets learned together, ate together, and slept together. There was no mother and father, only God the eternal Father and his son the divine Apostle. They were the cornerstone of his new church. A new Eden, and like Adam they had no need for shame. Girls did not go to school. They worked with their mothers, making meals and cleaning shit, until one or two or all of The Five were ready to usher them into glorious womanhood.

Three new men joined The Five to bring it back to five. All were sixteen, and all were hungrier below their pants than above. Brother Jakes had refused to give up his spot, despite being blind in both eyes. There was nothing he could do; leaving his house was dangerous, with an obstacle at every turn. He was at the mercy of others now, and his wife, faithful to the last, served him fritters the way he liked, along with chicken foot pumpkin soup. She served him as a dutiful wife should. And when she had her children spit or piss in the soup or had the oldest scoop up dried dog shit to mix with the fritter batter, all Brother Jakes's mind saw was devotion.

The fence was finished. It was not as high as Jericho, but high enough to convince outsiders not to trespass. The bridge was gone and the river grew violent and impassable. Soon, vines, leaves, and flowers attacked the wood and barbed wire with malignance and consumed the fence. Old villages disappeared from new maps often, whether they chose to or not. Within the fence no soul was hungry. They met as one in the church, sat in the pews, and drank porridge that the women made from ground corn. All water now came from the river, which ran though holes dug near the fence.

The Five had the hand of judgment. Mrs. Smithfield complained of being sick and tired of corn porridge. She scowled as she swallowed the last glob of slop and scowled all the way back home and through women's service. News of her displeasure had not even reached the Apostle before The Five paid her a visit. She never grumbled again. She never walked without a cane either.

Sunlight teased his nose and he awoke. Clarence climbed out of bed and went to the window. They lived at the Garvey house now, after The Five purged it of all iniquity. The French windows now had no curtains. Sunrays rushed into the room and he bathed in light. The day before, he saw four of The Five march through the gates carrying a boy and a girl, both no more than fourteen. He ran downstairs. The study was already closed and bolted from the inside. Clarence pressed his ear against the door but heard nothing.

He knew what would happen. Two more children. This was the second time in two months. The first two were a boy and girl as well, caught as they tried to climb over the fence. They were disciplined. The Apostle would not tolerate defiance, especially from the young, especially after God said suffer the children to come to Me. "Married? Married?" Clarence heard the mocking tone of the Apostle. Clarence could not make out any more words but he knew the sounds. They came as no surprise, the Apostle had a method for everything. The boy's cry was expected. There was only one place on a boy's body that when hit, he would cry like a girl. The girl's cry was expected, long and loud at first, then long and quiet after two, three, or four punches. Tony Curtis would rape her first, his ape yelps drowning her scream. Brother Patrick, after discovering how tight an anus was, would leave her vagina to the sixteen-year-olds. The rebellious boy would watch, learn, and be saved. The Apostle would tell them they only need one love—for God and His servant the Apostle.

Saved. The word brought Clarence back to the present, the light, the room, and the Apostle, snoring under purple sheets.

He had to piss. Clarence walked out of the room, leaving the door open. The bathroom was two doors ahead. He pissed, flicked himself, and turned to go back, when looking down he saw blood on the floor. Blood, but also slime in the shape of his foot. He looked up and there were more footprints, all with blood and slime that mingled but did not mix. He sat down on the toilet and lifted his right foot to see wet sores. When he rose, there was blood on the seat.

Outside, dust flew forward and dust flew back.

Syphilis, the great imitator, is a symphony in four movements. Like religion, it has no being in itself, but lives in the lives it touches. Like a God or a Devil. There are four movements. The first exists mostly in darkness, hiding more than showing. A spot on the anus, a lesion on the vagina, a corpuscle in the mouth that vanishes as quickly as a miracle. The third movement hides deeper than the first, waiting low in the flesh until time to rise again. The fourth movement comes with madness and blindness, consumption and illness of the breath. This is the trinity. One with soul and body after mind has been rotted. But the second movement is the one that leaves a trail.

A trail of blood and slime oozed from the puss-filled sores on Clarence's legs and feet. He had thought they were spots or scratches from the birds that were not healing quickly. Clarence ran back into the bedroom gasping, but stopped when he saw the Apostle, who sat up waiting on the bed.

"This is not death, this is life," the Apostle said. "This is not death. This is life. Any man who believes in me shall never die."

Clarence's head spun. He trusted the Apostle to be the center, not the spinner. His bloody footprints seemed to be walking by themselves, around the room in circles upon circles.

"Any man who believes in me shall never die."

Before the Apostle, Clarence was never really religious, not even when he went to the altar as he always did. God was something learned, never felt. The Apostle taught him new worship at the altar of the human body, communion with sweat and semen. But there was one lesson from church that he now remembered. One thing that the Apostle had said that he never truly believed. Clarence had not noticed this before, for he had no reason to say it himself. But his own blood brought the word back, sparking memory of another's blood, pricked from the rib with a spear. A name that was erased from Gibbeah with ease. He looked at the Apostle, who was already stroking himself and said, "Jesus."

The Apostle choked.

"Jesus."

"Don't say that word! Don't say that fucking word!"

"Jesus."

The Apostle rolled out of bed, yelling. He covered his ears and tried to run but tripped on a bloody, slimy footprint.

"Jesus."

"Stop it! Stop it! Stop it! I am the Messiah! I am the way, the truth, and the—"

"Jesus."

The Apostle writhed on the floor. He was still screaming when Clarence walked over to him. The Apostle's hands swung wildly, fighting off the spirits that he used to control.

"Jesus," Clarence said again, and watched the Apostle shake. Clarence grabbed the lamp from the table beside the bed and removed the shade. He swung high and clobbered the Apostle in the face. He struck him again and again, smashing his eye back into his skull, bursting his bottom lip, breaking his nose, and cracking the back of his head. The Apostle put up little resistance. Clarence bludgeoned him until his hand fell tired, until the Apostle's blood consumed him, until York's skull crushed soft, like a pumpkin. Then he bludgeoned him until the lamp broke. Blood was splattered all over Clarence's skin. It was a new baptism.

"Jesus," he said.

THE BEGINNING

The Apostle had not been seen in two days. The rest of The Five believed Clarence when he said that York wanted to rest and not be disturbed, but were surprised when he did not show up for the School of Boy Prophets, given his special interest in children. The village was surprised as well. Clarence knew what was coming. He bolted the door and laid the Apostle in the bathtub filled with water. The water was bloody, soaking the Apostle's body with crimson. His beautiful face was gone. Clarence wanted to die, but he wanted to live as well. The Five would most certainly kill him once they found out. But he was already dying.

Perhaps he and the Apostle could stay in the room forever. York had known him for who he truly was, and there was nothing to go back to now but lies. He heard a murmur in the wind. As Clarence looked out the window, he saw the crowd, the people of Gibbeah, gathered outside the house. He went to the bathroom. Any minute now The Five would kick down the door and kill him for what he had done. Clarence climbed into the tub, laid on top of the Apostle, the only living thing he ever loved, and embraced him. The Apostle sank underneath crimson water and Clarence sank underneath too.

The people wanted answers. It was not like the Apostle to leave his flock unattended for two days. Tony Curtis stood at the gate while Brother Patrick went toward the door. Just then a woman screamed. The crowd panicked and several fled. On the gate landed a dove, right beside Tony Curtis, who also ran, yelping in terror.

But not everyone left. There were a few who remembered that a dove was a bird of promise, not judgment. The dove flew and they followed his flight, running along Brillo Road until they came to the fence, which was covered in greenery. The river roared as the bird flew over to the other side. Through the spaces between leaves they saw the other side as well. They saw judgment and redemption, rescue and damnation, despair and hope.

She was dressed in a long, light blue dress and men's work boots laced up to her calves. She wore a wide straw hat that blocked the glare of the sun, but not the view of her face. As the wind whipped itself up and her dress blew like waves, the Widow raised her right hand and pointed two fingers.